Crazy About You

"This is terrific!" said Angie. "You are such a great guy!" She leaned over and kissed him.

Kissed him on the lips.

She pulled sharply away, realizing what she had just done. Without even thinking. Realizing that it had just felt like the most natural thing to do in the world. Realizing that it was what she had wanted to do for days...

What was it Steph had once said to her? Something about how she thought Peter Markowska was the most insufferable man she had ever met. Pompous, arrogant, and self-opinionated. And that how, one day, she realized that it was all an act to hide the shy and frightened man underneath.

She'd said something about opposites attracting.

Something about magnets and iron.

Point Romance

Crazy About You

Robyn Turner

Cover illustration by
Derek Brazzell

■ SCHOLASTIC

Scholastic Children's Books
Scholastic Publications Ltd,
7–9 Pratt Street, London NW1 0AE, UK

Scholastic Inc.,
555 Broadway, New York, NY 10012-3999, USA

Scholastic Canada Ltd,
123 Newkirk Road, Richmond Hill,
Ontario, Canada L4C 3G5

Ashton Scholastic Pty Ltd,
PO Box 579, Gosford, New South Wales,
Australia

Ashton Scholastic Ltd,
Private Bag 94407, Greenmount, Auckland,
New Zealand

First published by Scholastic Publications Ltd, 1995

ISBN 0 590 55803 X

Typeset by TW Typesetting, Midsomer Norton, Avon
Printed by Cox & Wyman Ltd, Reading, Berks.

Contents

1

December

The snow fell softly around Astor College, covering the sports fields in a crisp covering of white, and transforming the school's rolling grounds and old stone buildings into a scene from a Victorian Christmas card.

It was late afternoon, and already dark; inside the brightly-lit centrally-heated classrooms there was a feeling of well-earned indolence. After all, it was nearly Christmas and there were only two days to go before the end of term. If you couldn't start to slow down a bit before Christmas, then when could you?

The large school and sixth-form college in the Midlands, built on the site of a former country mansion for the landed gentry, had a reputation for turning out some of the best and brightest students in the entire country.

You certainly didn't need money to go to Astor College, even though the parents of many of the college's students were very well-off indeed, but you did need brains, and something which the teaching staff and the Board of Governors – self-made men and women every one of them – valued even more.

Individualism, thinking for yourself, standing on your own two feet – or stubbornness and sheer bloody-mindedness as some were inclined to call it – was something which was positively encouraged at Astor College. School work was important, certainly, and nothing but the best possible grades were expected from each and every student; but preparation for adult life and work was deemed just as important and therefore there was a whole host of extra-curricular activities from which Astor students could choose.

At the end of the school day when the corridors were packed with students, only half of those students were in a rush to go home; the other half were off to work on the school paper, go to a rehearsal of the school's drama society, or help out in Astor's community care scheme at the nearby Cuttleigh Hall.

So immersed in her own thoughts was one tall dark-haired girl at the end of this particular day that she wasn't looking where she was going, and she collided into a fellow student, a pretty and petite blonde-haired girl. As they ran into each other, the pile of files and folders the dark-haired girl was carrying fell tumbling to the floor.

"Shoot!" cried the taller girl, and bent down to pick up the files and papers.

"Sorry, Angie," the blonde girl said, as she knelt down to help her friend gather up her papers.

Angie ran a hand through her short black hair, which she'd recently had cut into a stylish bob by one of the top hair stylists in town.

"It's not your fault, Bec," she said, and smiled ruefully. "If I stopped charging around Astor like a bat out of hell it wouldn't have happened."

"It is Christmas, you know," Rebecca said, handing the files over to her best friend. "You are allowed to take a little time off, wind down. That's what holidays are for."

Angie stood up, and smoothed the creases in her sharp deep-blue Katharine Hamnett suit. "You know that Christmas is the busiest time of the year for me," she reminded Bec. "For starters, there's revision for next term's exams—"

"Don't remind me," Rebecca said glumly. Christmas was supposed to be a time of goodwill to all men, but obviously no one had informed Old Mother Greystone, their maths teacher, when she had set them their holiday homework.

"And there's Cuttleigh Hall's New Year's Eve party," Angie continued. "You promised to help me out this year."

"I know," Rebecca said. In fact, she had secretly been wishing that Angie had forgotten about the promise she had made her in the summer, when the thought of helping to organize a party for the disabled kids at Cuttleigh Hall hadn't seemed so bad. Christmas and New Year were supposed to be times for enjoying yourselves, not for spending most of your time elbow-deep in someone else's jelly and custard!

"Plus there's stories to prepare for the

3

Recorder," Angie finished. "The New Year issue's due out in the first week of next term." She sighed theatrically and chuckled. "Holiday? What holiday?"

"Don't you ever rest, Angela Markowska?" Rebecca asked in a mock-stern voice. "Straight-A student, part-time charity and care worker, and assistant editor of the student newspaper. I mean, do you ever get time to do the things we normal people do – like eat?"

For a moment Angie looked serious. "Bec, if my grandad hadn't worked hard, and raised enough money to move his entire family out of Poland just after the end of the second world war, I might not be here now. My dad's family were poor: it's only through sheer hard work that we've got to where we are today – I don't want to waste the opportunity I've been given."

Rebecca nodded, taking Angie's point, but still giggled. "Where you are today?" she repeated. "Living in the posh house on the hill, and having so little free time that you don't even get the chance to use your father's credit cards? Now that's what I call a waste!"

Angie gave Rebecca a friendly cuff on the shoulder: it was a long-running argument between the two of them.

"Bec, next year when you're at university reading soppy Victorian love poetry—"

"Alongside some soppy Victorian love-god, I hope," Rebecca said dreamily, and even Angie smiled.

"When you're at university, I want to be working as a journalist," Angie continued, sounding a little too earnest for her own good. "And every hour I put in on the student newspaper, every minute I spend experiencing some of the social problems of this town, every moment I'm helping someone less fortunate than myself, is going to stand me in good stead. Think of it as a sort of work-experience."

"But you could walk into a reporter's job as easily as that," Rebecca said, clicking her fingers.

"And what gives you that idea?"

"Well, your dad," Rebecca replied. "He works for the BBC in Birmingham, doesn't he? He could pull a few strings for you, and the next thing you know you'd be reading the Nine O'Clock News on the telly!"

Angie shook her head. "No way. He says that if I want a job in journalism then I've got to get it myself, the hard way. The way he got his own job."

Rebecca pulled a face, as if to show that she didn't think much of Peter Markowska's refusal to help his only daughter, but Angie smiled.

"And of course, he's right," she said. "If I can't get a job on the strength of my own talents, and can only get one because of who my dad is, then I'm simply not good enough!"

"You're determined, Angie, I'll give you that," Rebecca said, and started walking with her down the corridor towards the Senior Common Room.

A couple of boys from the lower sixth wolf-whistled as they passed by. Angie ignored them snootily; Rebecca, on the other hand, winked flirtatiously back at them.

"You've got to be determined in this world," Angie opined. "You've got to recognize exactly what it is you want, and then go out there and get it."

"You sound exactly like some of our teachers!" Rebecca said, and mimicked the accent of one of the more earnest careers advisers at Astor. " 'Gang your ain gait, mae wee children, gang your ain gait!' "

"Shut it!" Angie said, and punched her playfully in the ribs, as they reached the Common Room.

"But you're right," Rebecca agreed enthusiastically. "I've decided what I want and I'm going to go right out there to get it!"

Angie sniggered: she knew exactly what was coming next. "So who is he this time, Bec?"

"He's six-feet-two, has just turned nineteen, has the bluest, biggest eyes in the whole universe, and the cutest curly hair you've ever seen," she said animatedly, without pausing for anything so boring as a breath. "He's studying Physics, Chemistry and Engineering at the technical college down the road, he drives a second-hand Metro, his dad's something in computers, and, Angie, he is simply the hunkiest and most gorgeous creature on the surface of this entire planet!"

"I don't suppose you've found out his name yet?" Angie asked sarcastically.

"Adrian Fowler," Rebecca said smugly. "I tell you, Angie, this is it, this guy is going to be the biggest love of my life!"

6

"And have you actually met this sex-god yet?" Angie asked practically.

Rebecca's face fell. "Well, no, not exactly..."

"I thought not," Angie said wisely, and grinned. Rebecca was always falling in love at the drop of a hat. *Come to think of it*, Angie realized, *Rebecca Penswick doesn't even need the hat!*

"And that's where you come in, my bestest, bestest friend!" Rebecca said, and took Angie's arm.

"I do?" Angie suddenly had a sinking feeling in her stomach. She'd done favours for Rebecca before, favours which had usually landed her in a whole lot of trouble.

"I'm helping you out with your charities over Christmas," Rebecca reminded her, "so you owe me. Adrian's going to be at the Christmas dance tonight. Come with me, will you?"

"Bec, I haven't got the time..." Angie began, and then smiled. Rebecca was looking at her pleadingly, like a cute little kid, deprived of her favourite teddy bear. Maybe Bec was right, maybe she did need to unwind just a little.

"Well, OK," Angie finally gave in, and Rebecca clapped her hands triumphantly. "But what about tickets?" she asked, sensibly. "I thought the dance had sold out weeks ago."

Like a conjurer pulling a rabbit out of a hat, Rebecca whipped a pair of tickets out of the back pocket of her Levis. In response to Angie's puzzled look she explained that she had bought them several weeks ago when they had first been put on sale. Then she had been planning to go to

7

the dance with Rod, a good-looking fellow student on Rebecca's English Literature course.

"I seem to remember you calling Rod the greatest love of your life only a couple of weeks ago," Angie mischievously reminded her friend.

"Puuh-*lease*!" Rebecca said and shuddered. "He had spots like you wouldn't believe..."

"You didn't seem to mind that when you were kissing each other by the lockers," Angie recalled. "You didn't come up for air for hours!"

Rebecca glowered at her best friend: Angie had an infuriating habit of always reminding her of her past mistakes. "Anyway, he was *sooooo* immature," she said loftily.

"He was two months younger than you!" Angie giggled.

"That's what I mean," Rebecca laughed, and then was suddenly serious again. "But believe me, Angie, Adrian is it!"

"Sure, Bec." Angie nodded her head, clearly not believing at all. She'd give Bec's infatuation with Adrian about two weeks, before her dizzy friend fell for some other hunk. Bec was always flighty and changeable, unlike the ever-dependent and determined Angie, and that was probably why they got on so well.

Angie had only ever had one serious relationship with a boy before and that had been with Guy, the son of one of her stepmother's friends. He'd been solid and reliable ("boring" and "stick-in-the-mud", Rebecca had called him), and they'd gone out together for almost two years before he moved down to London to study for his

8

accountancy exams. The split had been amicable, and although Angie had been out with a couple of boys since Guy, there had been no one she had really cared for enough to give up her work on the *Recorder*.

What was more, Angie had seen what happened when people embarked on heavy relationships in their final year of college: their grades inevitably went down, because they were spending more time with their beloved than studying for the all-important A-levels. Journalism was a tough enough profession to enter at the best of times: she didn't want to mess it all up by falling in love with some hunk and getting anything less than the straight As she always got.

"So I'll meet up with you tonight?" Rebecca asked, as she said goodbye to Angie, who had to go off to another class. "And Angie...?"

"Yes?"

"Adrian's mine, OK?"

Angie frowned, but nodded anyway, and walked away, promising to pick Rebecca up at half-past seven that night. As Rebecca watched her friend disappear, she smiled stoically to herself.

Life just wasn't fair, she thought. Here she was, Rebecca, chasing after all the boys at Astor (and admittedly catching quite a few of them), when Angie, who wasn't interested in a relationship at all, could have had any one of them she wanted.

One day, Rebecca knew, Angie was going to wake up and discover just how beautiful she really was, if she'd only loosen up on her ambition and planning for her future career.

Rebecca turned and entered the Senior Common Room. She had more important things to occupy her mind now, like what to wear for the dance tonight, and the best chat-up line to try out on Adrian. Who knows? She might even manage to fix Angie up with a date as well!

The throbbing beat from the latest chart-topping sounds reverberated through the assembly hall as Astor College's Christmas dance got into full swing. The hall had been decked out with bright silver bunting and balloons, which sparkled and twinkled in the strobe lights reflected off the giant mirror ball in the ceiling.

At the side of the main dance area tables had been set out, and people were sitting round them and gazing out on to the dance floor, to see who was dancing with who, and who had sneaked off together to some dark corner, to kiss under a strategically placed sprig of mistletoe.

At the far end of the hall, a bunch of teachers sat, looking distinctly uncomfortable and out-of-place. They were there to make sure that things didn't get too out of hand, although none of them had been vigilant enough to spot the carrier bags full of wine that several students had success-fully smuggled into the hall, to supplement the Cokes and soft drinks available at the bar.

It was almost nine o'clock now and the dance floor was packed with couples bopping and gyrating to the latest in disco, house and techno. Angie, dressed in a white Nicole Farhi top and trendy Calvins, was sitting at a table by herself, after having turned down the third invitation to dance in as many minutes.

She was scribbling in shorthand in a reporter's notebook, occasionally looking up to see Rebecca and Adrian dancing on the dance floor. Angie smiled to herself: her best friend hadn't wasted any time, and had been monopolizing the handsome college student for the best part of an hour.

The dance track faded, to be replaced by a sugary-sweet piece of nonsense from one of the latest Aussie soap stars, and Rebecca and Adrian left the dance floor in disgust, to rejoin Angie at her table. Rebecca glanced down at the notebook, unsuccessfully trying to decipher Angie's shorthand notes.

"Don't you ever stop!" she said and raised her eyes heavenwards in despair. She closed Angie's notebook for her, before reaching out for her plastic cup of red wine.

"Sorry!" Angie laughed guiltily. "I was working on some ideas for an article for the *Reporter*!"

"You should be out there on the dance floor, enjoying yourself," said Adrian, who, if not quite the love-god that Rebecca had described, was still extremely good-looking and very pleasant. He was showing more than a friendly interest in Angie too, Rebecca noticed; but then, so were most of the boys at the dance. Some girls had all the luck!

"Angie wants to become the next Lois Lane," Rebecca announced, and added pointedly: "And until she does she's not going to allow even Superman to get a look-in!"

"That's a shame," oozed Adrian. "And such a waste too…"

Rebecca listened in, horrified. *Was Adrian actually coming on to her best friend?*

"Look, why don't you two go back and dance?" Angie suggested tactfully as the DJ started to play a smoochy tune. "I'll be fine here."

"You're sure?" asked Adrian.

"Of course she's sure!" said Rebecca and grabbed Adrian's hand, dragging him back on to the dance floor.

Angie smiled as she watched them join the other couples who were swaying gently to and fro. The song was unfamiliar to her, sung by a deep male voice against some average male harmonies, telling of how the singer had known lots of girls but thought he'd never meet the right one.

It was pleasant enough, Angie thought, but a little too sentimental and slushy for her taste; it was probably just an attempt by another band of pretty boys to cash in on their good looks, and write a song which would appeal to all the pre-pubescent teenagers out there. She was far too grown-up to be taken in by all that pop-music hype!

"Would you like to dance to Zone with me, Angela?" asked a dark-brown voice above her.

Angie looked up to see the smiling face of Dominic Cairns, the captain of the college football team. They'd known each other by sight for a couple of years now, but had never really spoken to each other before.

"Excuse me?" said Angie. "Zone?"

"That's who's playing now," Dominic said. "They're a new band, and it's their first single."

Angie looked back at the dance floor: Rebecca and Adrian were getting involved in what looked like a pretty serious clinch. She felt a pang of envy.

"Well, I don't know..." she said unsurely.

"I'd be honoured if you did," Dominic smoothed. He smiled at her, displaying a set of dazzling white teeth. "It's so rare that I get a chance to dance with such an attractive girl..."

"Then how can I say no?" Angie said and allowed Dominic to take her hand and lead her out on to the dance floor.

As they passed through the throng of couples, Rebecca released herself from Adrian's passionate embrace, and her eyes glanced over at them.

So, for that matter, did the eyes of every other girl on the dance floor.

"Will you just look at that!" Rebecca said to her companion, as Angie and Dominic began to slow-dance in time to the sensual beat of Zone's first single. "Angie and Dominic Cairns!"

Adrian nuzzled Rebecca's neck. "So?" he asked, his mind obviously on much more interesting things. "What's the big deal?"

"The big deal is that Dominic is the most gorgeous, scrumptious boy in our entire school," she said. "He's the guy everyone says could make the big time as a male model if he wasn't captain of the football team."

Adrian grunted noncommittally, and returned to stroking the small of Rebecca's back, sending frissons of pleasure coursing down her spine. That was the trouble with boys, Rebecca thought ironically; they were only ever interested in one thing. They just didn't appreciate the delights of a good gossip.

"Every girl's been running after him for ... well, for ever. And who gets to dance with him without even trying?" Rebecca asked rhetorically. "What a lucky so-and-so Angie is! But I never even thought Dominic was interested in girls; the only thing he seems to have time for is kicking that football of his around. Adrian, this is the start of something big!"

Unaware of all the attention being focused on her, or the fact that she had suddenly become an item of envy for practically every girl in the room, Angie was enjoying herself immensely.

Despite his heavy football-player's build, Dominic was a surprisingly good dancer, leading her smoothly across the floor as if he had been doing it for years, and it felt good to have his body alongside hers. Beneath his open-necked cotton shirt she could feel his firm and strong pectoral muscles, and the biceps in his upper arms were hard and pumped. There was a hint of cologne about him: not one of those fancy and expensive foreign scents, but down-to-earth and masculine, making her think of rugged countryside and clear mountain streams.

Dominic looked down at her, fixing her with those brilliantly blue eyes which he knew could make almost all the girls at Astor weak at the knees.

"You're a very good dancer, Angela," he said approvingly.

"My mother taught me when I was a child," Angie replied, and held Dominic even more tightly. They weaved in and out of the other couples, and she ran her hand down the small of his back to the base of Dominic's spine, to the top of his smart Armani trousers. "She used to be a professional dancer – before she died."

"I'm sorry," said Dominic, and even sounded as though he meant it, Angie thought. Angie had always steered clear of Dominic before, distrusting his undeniably devastating good looks – *let the other girls giggle and make fools of themselves over him*, she had always told herself. But here on the dance floor, he seemed a very nice guy indeed, charming and modest, and blissfully unaware that he was probably the most handsome guy in the entire hall.

"You needn't be sorry, Dominic," she said. "Mum died a long time ago. And Stephanie – my dad's new wife – has been as good as a real mother to me…"

They danced in silence for a few moments, and Dominic pulled her closer to him. Angie looked up into his eyes: he really was most extraordinarily sexy, she decided, with thick dark hair, just curling over his collar, a firm jaw, and a swarthy Mediterranean complexion. Just her type, in fact; she hated pasty-faced blonds. She giggled.

"What's so funny?" Dominic asked, wanting to share in the joke.

"Bec was trying to fix me up with a date before," she said, wondering if the wine she had been drinking was starting to go to her head. "With some spotty fifth-former. She's convinced that I need a boyfriend for Christmas..."

"Well, I'm glad that she was unsuccessful," Dominic said, and then looked at her seriously. "And *do* you?" he asked.

"Do I what?" Angie said coyly, although she knew perfectly well what Dominic was asking her.

Near them, Rebecca and Adrian had manoeuvred themselves within listening distance: Rebecca had decided that this was going to be too good to miss out on!

"Need a boyfriend for Christmas?" Dominic breathed huskily.

A look passed between them, a look which said everything they needed to know. Thirty pairs of envious female eyes glared green with jealousy as the handsomest, sexiest and hunkiest guy at Astor Sixth-Form College bent his head down to kiss Angie.

Angie felt her heart pound in her breast, inhaled Dominic's warm and sexy smell, felt the taut muscles flex in his broad, strong back. Suddenly her entire world had become centred on this one spot on the dance floor. There was no one else here but her and Dominic, no other sound than the seductive and romantic tones of this new band, singing about the search for their one true love. It had been such a long and lonely time since Angie had allowed herself to be affected this way by any boy, and she realized now just how much she had missed it.

She closed her eyes, raising her head to meet Dominic's lips.

And then suddenly she broke away.

"Omigod!" she cried. "I'd forgotten all about it!"

"Angela, what is it?" asked Dominic, his voice full of concern. "Are you all right?"

Angie looked down at her Swatch. It was a quarter to ten. If she rushed she might just make it!

"Look, Dominic, I'm really, really sorry," she started to babble. "But the new Christmas hospice…"

"Christmas hospice?" Dominic was confused.

"Yeah, it's being opened tonight," she said. "By the Social Security Minister who's come up especially from London…"

"So?"

"Well, if I can get an interview with him for the *Reporter*, that would be a real scoop!" she said, and pushed her way through the smooching couples to the edge of the dance floor. She rushed over to her table, and grabbed her reporter's notebook, then turned to Dominic who had followed her.

"Look, I'm really sorry, Dominic," she said, and kissed him – a friendly peck on the cheek and not the long, deep and passionate kiss he had been expecting on the dance floor. "But you do understand, don't you?"

The look on Dominic's face made it plain that he didn't understand in the slightest. He was speechless: nothing like this had ever happened to him before. Usually he couldn't get rid of the girls: no one had ever walked out on him before!

"I'll make it up to you," Angie promised as she picked up her coat from the back of her chair, and the hapless Dominic helped her to put it on. She kissed him on the cheek again. "Have to dash now. See you!"

And with that Angie Markowska left the most gorgeous boy in the whole of Astor College standing alone, and rejected, and feeling more than a little puzzled and foolish, and raced out into the cold and biting winds of an English winter. Thirty girls who had been watching the whole scene decided that she was the biggest fool it had ever been their misfortune to know.

From the dance floor Rebecca and Adrian watched her go. Rebecca shook her head in amazement and, it has to be said, a little bit of perverse admiration. She turned to Adrian, who, in common with most of the boys present, wasn't quite sure what all the fuss was about.

"My best friend is the craziest, dumbest, most brain-dead person in the history of the world. Dumping Dominic Cairns for a fusty old Government Minister!"

"It's her job, so you were telling me," Adrian said.

"This is Christmas, Adrian," Rebecca replied. "We're allowed to switch off for the holiday season!"

"Angie doesn't seem to me to be the sort of girl who can switch off, or who does things by halves," decided Adrian. "Either she's going to go right to the very top in her career, or she's going to fall so head-over-heels in love that journalism is going to be the last thing on her mind!"

"You really think so?" asked Rebecca, and regarded her new boyfriend in a different light.

Not only was he a major hunk, the second cutest guy here tonight, but it sounded like he was also something of a secret romantic.

"Sure," he said, and then added: "And on that day you're going to see pigs flying in close formation over Astor College. Now come on, Bec, and let's dance!"

2

"You do know I'm mortally ashamed to be your friend, Angie Markowska?" Rebecca announced loudly the following morning. She had met up with Angie in the offices of the school newspaper, where Angie had spent most of the morning typing up a story on one of the paper's two Apple Macs.

"Yeah, that's the third time you've told me –" Angie looked up at the digital clock on the wall – "in twenty minutes."

She glanced down at her spiral-bound notepad to check up on a fact and then, satisfied that her article was as perfect as she could make it, pressed the "Command-S" keys to save it on the hard disk, and started to print it out on the laser printer.

She swivelled around in her chair to look at her friend. "Look, Bec, what's the big problem?"

"What's the big problem?" Rebecca couldn't believe what she was hearing. "The big problem is that you dump Dominic Cairns at the Christmas party!"

"So?" asked Angie, and smiled fondly as she

recalled the special way she had felt in Dominic's arms. "What's so brilliant about Dominic Cairns? He's only the captain of the football team, after all."

Rebecca sighed: her best friend could be so dim at times.

"Angie, it may have escaped your notice but Dominic Cairns is not just the captain of the school football team. He's also SuperHunk, Sex On Legs, the guy most girls at Astor would kill their grandparents for! They say that some national magazine is even interested in him doing some modelling for them, so gorgeous-looking is he. And you went and left him standing there! The official verdict is that you are seriously off your head!"

Angie shrugged, but couldn't help but be amused – and more than a little flattered – by all the commotion she seemed to have caused by ditching Dominic last night.

"I'm a journalist, Bec, or at least I hope to be one some day," she reminded her loftily. "I had a story to get!"

"And did you?" Rebecca asked pointedly.

Angie laughed ironically. "The Social Security Minister didn't make it in the end," she admitted. "Got caught up in the snow. Some boring old councillor opened up the Hospice instead!"

"See!" Rebecca crowed. "So it was all a waste of time after all! If you'd've listened to me you could have stayed with Dominic last night, and this morning you'd be the envy of every single female in the world!"

"You know something, Bec?" Angie laughed. "You're obsessed with men!"

Rebecca nodded happily. "Adrian – you know the guy I met last night?"

"How could I forget?" Angie asked sarcastically. "You haven't stopped talking about him!"

"Adrian is just one of the most wonderful guys in the world," Rebecca oozed. "Kind, gentle, intelligent, and so good-looking it just isn't true!"

"That's what you said about Rod," Angie reminded her, laughing. "And the one before him. And the one before him…"

Rebecca stuck her tongue out at her: Angie was always reminding Rebecca about her past boyfriends. It wasn't her fault that they didn't last so long; there was always someone just a little bit cuter, just a little sexier for Rebecca to fall head-over-heels in love with. Adrian, she was sure however, was going to be different.

"At least I go out with boys," she said sulkily. "Unlike you – always chasing after the next big story."

"I have been known to go out with boys too, you know," Angie reminded her best friend.

"Guy? That was over almost twelve months ago," Rebecca said. She looked seriously at Angie. "Listen, Angie, we're seventeen. In another couple of years we're both going to be over the hill. We've got to have fun now while we can and before it's too late!"

She sauntered over to the editor's desk, which was littered with computer disks, bulging ring-binder files, and press releases. One press release in particular, paper-clipped to a glossy black-and-white photo, caught her eye, and she snatched it up. She rapidly scanned the press release, which had been sent to the paper's offices by a small record company based about a hundred miles away in Manchester.

"Zone are coming to town?" she asked. "I don't believe it!"

Angie, who was tidying up some files at her own desk, shrugged. "Zone? Who are Zone?" she asked.

"You danced to them last night!" Rebecca reminded her and gazed down at the seven-by-eight glossy. "When Dominic Dreamboat dragged you out on the dance floor!"

"Oh, yeah, I remember," Angie said and smiled. Dominic's body had been so warm and comfortable pressed up against hers. "So who are they?"

Rebecca passed over the photo for Angie to take a look. Angie nodded wisely to herself: she had been right last night when she guessed that the four guys in the band were a bunch of opportunists who were banking that their pretty-boy looks would take the place of talent and make them into stars.

Rebecca sighed, and pretended to swoon. "Zone are just the best band ever to have appeared on the scene in the past twenty years," she enthused.

"So why haven't I heard of them?" Angie asked. "Before last night, that is."

"They only formed a few months ago," Rebecca explained knowledgeably. "That was their first single – "Lost Without You" – that you heard last night."

Angie smiled and handed the photo back to Rebecca, who gazed dreamily at it. "So if they've only released one track, how come you think they're the greatest band in the world?" she asked, although she had a pretty good idea of what Rebecca's answer would be.

Rebecca shook her head sadly: if Angie was going to ask such stupid questions she was going to be middle-aged before she even reached twenty! "Angie, with looks like these boys have got, they're bound to be big!"

"Far too pretty for me," Angie said dismissively. She remembered Dominic's rugged handsomeness. She could certainly imagine him as a model, perhaps advertising a new brand of jeans, all tough and masculine. Maybe she'd been wrong last night to ditch him for that non-existent scoop.

"Pretty? *Pretty?*" Rebecca scoffed. "Calling these guys pretty is like saying the Sistine Chapel is kind of nice. These guys are to die for!" She pointed out the individual members of the band one by one.

"That's Danny," she said, pointing to a cute Italian-looking guy, dressed in a trendy T-shirt, designer-ripped 501s and a back-to-front baseball cap. "He plays drums and does backing vocals."

Angie nodded: in the photo Danny was trying to look tough, but with his baby-face it wasn't quite working. He looked about seventeen which made him, Angie guessed, at least two or three years younger than the other members of the band.

Rebecca indicated a black boy, whose baggy linen shirt had been undone to his waist, displaying his muscular torso to his adoring female fans.

"That's Marco – he plays bass guitar – and this mean and moody hunk with the designer stubble is Luke on keyboards…"

Angie then pointed to the fourth member of the group, who was standing in the foreground, removed from the other band members. He was tall, dressed in black leathers, and a white muscle shirt. He had dishevelled blond hair, which Angie immediately (and correctly) suspected hadn't been washed for a few days, and which curled over the collar of his leather biker's jacket; there was a tiny crucifix-shaped earring hanging in his right ear.

Angie found herself instantly disliking him: this guy oozed attitude, with a capital "A", and looked as though he had an over-inflated opinion of himself too. Even so, he dominated the photograph and it was hard to take her eyes off him.

"And who's this?" she asked casually, trying not to give away just how interested she was.

"I've left the best to last!" said Rebecca, sounding just like a star-crazy, love-struck schoolkid. "That's JJ, Zone's lead singer. He writes all their songs too. Isn't he the hunkiest thing you've ever seen in your life?"

"I wouldn't let Adrian hear you say that!" Angie advised her. "And what sort of name is JJ anyway?"

Rebecca shrugged, and picked up the press release again. "No one knows," she said, and then suddenly had a great idea. "Hey, Angie, you think you're such a good reporter! Why don't you try and find out?"

"Somehow I don't think discovering the real identity of a second-rate pop singer is going to get me a job on the local paper when I leave school," Angie replied.

God, did that really sound as pompous as I think it did? she immediately asked herself.

Rebecca finished scanning the press release. "You'd have no chance anyway," she told her flatly.

"And why's that?" Angie asked.

"The boys are coming to play at the local town hall – I must get some tickets," Rebecca said, reading from the press release. "But there's a strict ban on interviews. No one is allowed to get near them, not even the national papers. As far as the Press is concerned Zone are strictly off-limits."

Angie grabbed the sheet of paper from Rebecca, and read it more closely. There was an eager and challenged look in her blue eyes.

"Off-limits, are they?" she said scornfully. "We'll see about that!"

Rebecca looked at her best friend warily. She might have known: if something was forbidden to Angie Markowska then she went right out there and got it.

Rebecca recognized the gleam in Angie's eyes. She had seen it once before, a couple of years ago when Angie had been going out with Guy. Her grades had fallen off and Mrs Greystone had given her a severe telling-off in front of the rest of the maths class. The teacher had told Angie that her recent string of Cs wasn't acceptable, and that she had better start improving her work.

Determined to prove the teacher wrong, Angie had set about her work with a determination that was almost frightening: the next term she got nothing less than perfect As for every single one of her papers.

If Angie Markowska wanted something then she usually got it. Zone had better watch out!

What was the point of having a father when he didn't help you out when you needed him the most? Angie asked herself later that evening. She had returned home, through the snow, to ask her dad one tiny favour, and he'd turned away and told her in no uncertain terms that he had no intention of doing any favours for her at all, no matter how small.

Angie turned away angrily from her father and stamped her feet in frustration. Peter Markowska was a still good-looking man of fifty-one, and the greatest dad in the world, Angie knew; he was also one of the most stubborn, irritating and pig-headed adults she had ever known!

"Come on, Dad," she pleaded. "I've tried every other way I can think of. I've rung their record company, their management company, I've even bought a ticket for their concert! But there's no way that I can get an interview with Zone!"

Her dad smiled, and shook his head sympathetically. "Then you'll just have to be philosophical about the whole thing and accept that you can't interview Zone," he said.

Angie, however, wasn't prepared to be "philosophical" about anything. "If I got an exclusive interview with them, I could sell it to the papers!" she said. "It would look so good on my CV – the only reporter in the country to get an interview with the most up-and-coming boy-band around. And not just any reporter but a school reporter at that!"

"I know it would," her father agreed. "I'm sure the local paper would be interested in it – after all, even though they're based in Manchester now, Zone do come from this area. I imagine they'd love an exclusive story about the local boys made good..."

Angie looked curiously at her fifty-one-year-old dad: she hadn't thought that he would know something like that: she'd only found out that all four members of the band were local guys when Rebecca had told her.

"Oh, I keep an open mind," he said, in response to her unspoken question.

"You could help me, Dad," Angie continued.

Her father gave her a look as if to say *Oh, can I now?* and Angie continued.

"You work in TV, Dad, everyone says that you're one of the best TV arts producers around!"

Peter smiled but didn't say anything: after all, having worked for almost thirty years on late-night arty TV programmes, he'd been flattered by experts!

"You know everyone who is anyone," Angie

reminded him. "You could use your connections, pull a few strings. If anyone could get me an interview with Zone you could!"

Peter glanced down at the press release Angie had brought home with her. "I probably could," he agreed, and read the name of Zone's management company, which was printed at the foot of the sheet of paper. "Krupp Promotionals." The name rang a bell, and he cast his mind back a few years.

"I met Joe Krupp once, just before your mother died. He was interested in signing her up for a dance special on TV. I've probably still got his phone number somewhere in my Filofax."

"Then you'll help me?" Angie asked. "You'll phone up Joe Krupp?" She leaned over and kissed her father gratefully on the cheek. "Oh, Dad, you're the best dad in the world and I know you're going to be so proud of me when you see my interview printed in the papers!"

Peter shook his head. "No, darling, I'm not going to help you," he stated firmly.

"*What?*" Angie couldn't believe what her dad was saying.

"If you want your interview with Zone, then that's fine by me," he said, and stood up from his chair. "But get it yourself. If you're really cut out to be a reporter then you'll be able to interview Zone without my help."

"But—"

"Sorry, darling," her dad said, "you're on your own on this one."

He walked out of the room.

"Of all the pig-headed, arrogant, selfish, old-fashioned—" Angie spluttered.

She turned to Stephanie, her dad's second wife, who had been silently following the conversation from her armchair. Stephanie was a research physicist at the local University. She was several years younger than Angie's dad and Angie often regarded her as an older sister rather than a stepmother. The fact that she wore her ash-blonde hair in a short and trendy bob made her look even younger.

"Can you believe that, Steph?" she said. "How can he be so cruel?"

Stephanie put down the research papers she had been working on, and patted the chair next to her, indicating that Angie should sit down and talk to her.

"He's only got your best interests at heart, Angie," she said. "And deep down you know he's right."

Angie sighed. "I suppose so," she admitted reluctantly. "But an interview with Zone would be so good for me."

"Then go for it," Stephanie said. "Prove to your dad that you can do it. Prove it to yourself."

"Security around Zone is so tight I'd have a better chance of breaking into the Bank of England," Angie said glumly. "If only that so-and-so had agreed to help me!"

Stephanie chuckled. "That so-and-so is your dad – my husband – who's only interested in your welfare. If it's any consolation I'd happily give you Joe Krupp's telephone number," she said.

"You have his number too?" Angie asked, immediately hoping that Stephanie would prove an ally in her attempt to secure an interview.

"Well, yes – on my computer," Stephanie said. "You know how absent-minded your dad is. I'm sure that one day he's going to lose that Filofax of his, so I had him copy all his important phone numbers on to my hard disk for safe-keeping." She paused, considered, then added hastily: "On second thoughts, don't ask me for the number – not even I'm prepared to face your father's wrath!"

Angie laughed. "Thanks anyway," she said. "At least you're different from the Dad from Hell..."

"Different?" Stephanie smiled.

"Yeah," Angie said. "You don't always push me to the limits like Dad does. You're much more easy-going." She indicated the sheaf of papers Stephanie was working on. They were filled with numbers and symbols which Angie knew she'd never have a hope of understanding. "You even have a totally different gobbledygook!"

Stephanie laughed. "That 'gobbledygook' is my work!" she said. "As far as I'm concerned, all the arty novels and intellectual films your dad reviews are gobbledygook to me!"

"But you're both so different," Angie said. "I mean, for most of the time Dad goes around with his head in the clouds, talking about literature, and black-and-white foreign films, and classical music and dance. And you go on about quarks and anti-quarks, and protons and neutrons and tau-mesons and a thousand other things I don't understand."

Stephanie chuckled. "The only difference is that your father deals with the abstract, and I look after the concrete," she said. "What more perfect match could there be?" She smiled again. "But what you really mean, Angie, is that I'm different from your real mother..."

Angie turned away shyly, uncomfortable at the direction the conversation was taking. "It's just that my dad and my mum were always interested in the same things," she said. "When they met she was training to be a classical dancer and he was a trainee arts producer for the BBC. They moved in the same circles, went to the same concerts and ballets and films, and they just seemed so right together, so perfect for each other..."

"Meaning I'm not?" asked Stephanie mischievously.

"Oh, I don't mean that!" Angie said and turned back to her stepmother. "You know I love you, Steph, and I'm really glad that you and Dad got together after my mum died." She lowered her eyes, so as not to look Stephanie in the face. "But you'll never take the place of my real mum..."

"I don't intend to," Stephanie said gently. "Your mother was a very special person for you, and your father, and no one can ever replace her."

"You make Dad happy, and that makes me happy too," Angie said. "But if someone had told me that you and he were going to get together, I'd never have believed it! I mean, how many times have you been to see *The Nibelungenlied*, or watched a scratchy copy of an arty-farty French movie on late-night telly?"

"Never," Stephanie admitted cheerfully. "But then how many times has your father discussed the logistical and ethical problems of nuclear fission or questioned the validity of Einstein's theory of relativity?"

"Point taken."

"Opposites do attract sometimes, Angie," Stephanie said. "And three years ago, if someone had told me that I would end up marrying your father I would have thought that they were crazy too. The first time I met him I thought he was pompous, arrogant, conceited, and much too full of himself."

"You're not far wrong there," Angie said cheekily.

Stephanie chose to ignore her stepdaughter's remark and continued: "But as I got to know him better I found that that was only the impression he gave to the world because he was shy about meeting other people."

"Dad? Shy?"

Stephanie nodded. "His stand-offish manner was just a front, a form of self-defence, if you like, for those times he was confronted with people like me who he didn't know what to make of," she explained. "But as I got to know him better I discovered that he was the sweetest, gentlest, most lovable man I had ever known in my life. And, in spite of all our differences, soon I found myself falling helplessly in love with him.

"Love's like that, Angie: it's got no prejudices, it

never plays by the rules. You might have known someone for years, and have never felt anything for them; you might not even be able to stand that person, or at the very least think that they're not your type; and then suddenly little old Cupid goes and fires his arrow, and – well, you know the rest..."

Angie thought about this for a second and then laughed. " 'Little old Cupid and his arrow?' " she said flippantly, and pulled a face of mock-disgust. "That's the sort of slushy nonsense my dad might come out with! You're learning from him, Steph!"

"Not as much as he's learning from me," Steph said, joining in the joke. "Why, only the other day I caught him trying to mend the washing machine! This from the man who had to be told only a couple of months ago how to wire a plug!"

"Now that really is something!" Angie remarked.

"When two opposites meet they learn from each other," Stephanie said. "And the most important thing you learn is that, no matter what your superficial differences are, you can never stay apart for long. It's no use fighting the attraction: you're drawn to each other like a magnet is to a piece of iron.

"All you can do is give in. If you don't, if you struggle against it, then you're going to be miserable for the rest of your life. And I, for one, am glad that I didn't fight against that attraction..."

"And I'm glad too," said Angie, and gave

Stephanie a daughterly peck on the cheek. She looked towards the door through which her father had left. "He's still the Dad from Hell though!"

Stephanie burst out laughing as her step-daughter lightened the tone of the conversation. "He's your father, and he wants to look after you!" she repeated.

"If he's interested in my welfare he could have got me my interview!" she said lightly.

"Like he said, this is your chance to prove what a crack reporter you are," Stephanie said. "And besides, maybe there's another reason for him not wanting you to get the interview..."

"And what's that?" asked Angie, suddenly serious.

"Well, you're his only daughter and he loves you more than anything else in this world," the older woman said, with a wicked twinkle in her eye. "And you know what they all say about rock stars, don't you...?"

"No," Angie said, all coyly, and grinned as she put her stepmother on the spot. "What do they all say about rock stars, Steph?"

Stephanie was about to answer when the telephone rang. She answered it, and passed the cordless receiver over to Angie.

"Hello?" Angie frowned, wondering who could be asking for her at half-past eleven at night.

"Angie, is that you?"

Rebecca's voice crackled down the receiver. In the background Angie could hear the buzz of people talking and the throbbing rhythms of some heavy house and techno music: she remembered Rebecca telling her that Adrian had promised to take her to the town's trendiest and most happening club tonight, and guessed that that was where Rebecca was phoning her from.

"Listen, I told you that Adrian was a catch and a half, didn't I?" Rebecca said excitedly, shouting to make herself heard above the sound of the techno beat.

"He's a nice guy, Bec," Angie agreed, smiling to herself. Rebecca was always like this in the first few days of a new relationship, ringing everyone up to tell them just how wonderful her current boyfriend was: she'd calm down in a few days' time, after the first flush of "love" had faded away.

"We have just had the most fantastic conversation ever," Rebecca continued.

"I'm surprised you can hear him above all that noise," Angie joked.

"We've learned so much about each other," Rebecca said. "He's kind, he's charming, he's intelligent and witty—"

On the other end of the line, Angie nodded impatiently. "All your boyfriends are, Bec. What's so special about him?"

"Listen, Angie, we got talking about our families, right?" Rebecca said, determined to make Angie wait as long as possible for her devastating piece of gossip. "I told him all about how my brother's two-timing *his* girlfriend..."

For Heaven's sake, Bec, get to the point! Angie thought irritably.

"And Angie, you are never in a million years going to guess who Adrian's cousin is!"

From her armchair Stephanie watched Angie's expression turn into one of delighted incredulity as Rebecca announced her news.

"Adrian is related to *who*?" Angie asked down the phone. She could scarcely believe her good luck. She glanced over to Stephanie and, with her free hand, gave her a thumbs-up gesture of victory.

Her exclusive interview with the four guys from Zone was as good as guaranteed!

3

The thuggish-looking bouncer, who was wearing a black T-shirt and black leather trousers, looked down at the backstage pass Angie had presented him with. He studied it carefully – *probably because he's only just learned how to read joined-up writing*, Angie thought rather uncharitably – and then he glanced back up at Angie's anxious face. Angie gulped, wondering whether he would see past her deception.

She was dressed in a leather jacket to protect her against the cold, a loose-fitting Katharine Hamnett blouse, and well-cut blue jeans, which she imagined made her look sophisticated and self-assured, and not at all like the giggling schoolkids who were gathered around the stage door of Astor Town Hall, in the hope of catching a glimpse of their pop-star heroes. Even though it was bitterly cold and snowing they had been huddled outside for hours now. In Angie's shoulder bag was a small tape recorder and a list of questions that she and Rebecca had thought of that morning to ask the boys from Zone.

The bouncer regarded her through narrow, suspicious eyes. "A. Fowler," he read from the pass. His breath hung in clouds in front of his mouth. "And that's supposed to be you?"

"That's right," she said nervously and shivered in the cold. "Angela Fowler."

It had been Rebecca's idea to use Adrian's backstage pass; after all, Adrian, who had unexpectedly had to visit some old maiden aunt with his Christmas presents, wouldn't be able to use it.

Angie gulped: this sort of thing always looked so easy on TV, but it was a lot more hair-raising in real life. Was the bouncer going to believe her? Or was he going to turn her away like she had already seen him turn away scores of fans desperate to get backstage for a chance to speak to their idols?

The bouncer obviously wasn't convinced. "You got any other ID?" he asked gruffly.

Aha! Angie thought triumphantly. *You thought you'd catch me out on that, didn't you!*

She beamed and rooted in her bag for her school press pass. She passed it to the bouncer who read it and checked Angie's photo in the top right-hand corner. He shrugged.

"Angela Fowler," he read again. "Seems like you're on the level after all."

Angela gave herself a congratulatory pat on the back. She'd guessed that the bouncer would have needed some additional ID to identify her as "A. Fowler", so she had spent the afternoon producing a fake press card in that name on one of the *Recorder*'s Apple Macs.

Lois Lane, eat your heart out! she crowed to herself. *They don't call me an ace reporter for nothing!*

The bouncer handed the backstage pass and the fake ID back to Angie. "So you're Luke's cousin, are you?" he grinned, his manner now much more friendly as he realized that Angie wasn't a pushy fan or a tiresome groupie.

"That's right," she breezed. "Luke and me, we're like that." She crossed her fingers together to illustrate her point – and for luck.

The bouncer stroked his chin which was covered with a few days' beard growth. "Funny he never mentioned you before, though," he said. "He's always been one for the girls, has our Luke. I'm sure he would have mentioned someone as pretty as you…"

Good grief, he isn't coming on to me, is he? Angie asked herself in disbelief. *This bouncer's almost old enough to be my dad!* She laughed nervously. "I … er, I like keeping a low profile."

"Sure," said the bouncer who still hadn't let her inside. "I suppose you've met the other boys as well?"

Angie nodded. "Naturally," she said. "We're all great pals. We see each other all the time. Marco. Danny. And, of course, EJ."

"JJ," the bouncer corrected her.

"Yeah, that's right, JJ…" Angie said, and kicked herself.

The bouncer looked at her for a few more seconds, eyeing her up, Angie thought … and then stood aside.

"OK," he said, "go in!"

Done it! Angie whooped to herself. *Pulled the wool over your eyes well and good! Scoop of the year, here I come!*

She skipped lightly past the bouncer and started to head off down the corridor to where he had told her the boys' dressing room was. Suddenly a short, fat man emerged from an open doorway, as silently as a cat, and Angie ran straight into him.

"I'm sorry," she said, and looked up at the man's podgy face. He had piggy eyes, and a narrow, unpleasant mouth; he reminded Angie of the baddies she had seen on some of the late-night trashy movies she and Stephanie loved to watch.

"And who have we here?" the man asked, looking not at Angie but at the bouncer standing by the open door.

"Angela Fowler, boss," the bouncer said. "She says she's Luke's cousin."

"Indeed?" The fat man stared down at Angie, a look of disbelief on his ugly face. Angie dived into her bag again and pulled out her backstage pass.

"See?" she said, pushing the card under the fat man's pug nose. "A. Fowler – Access All Areas."

The fat man took Angie's arm – a little too roughly – and marched her towards the door. Angie shook him off.

"I've got to see my cousin," she protested. "He's expecting me…"

"Luke is not expecting you, nor is any other one of my boys," the fat man said roughly.

He grabbed Angie's backstage pass and tore it

in half and threw it on to the floor. "You are also not Luke's cousin – unless you have recently had a sex change which I have not been informed about! Luke's cousin is called Adrian, not Angela—"

Angie's face fell, but she was still determined to stick to her story. "How come you know so much about Luke's family?" she asked the fat man defiantly, as the bouncer marched up to escort her out.

"My name is Joe Krupp and I am the manager of Zone," the fat man announced. "And I make it my business to know everything about my boys. Now, goodbye, Ms Fowler – or whatever your real name is!"

The bouncer escorted Angie unceremoniously out of the theatre and back into the cold. The fans who had been waiting outside gave her sympathetic looks: it had been a nice try, but didn't she know that Joe Krupp was famous for making sure that no one ever intruded on his clients without his written permission? That was why he was one of the most successful managers in the business: he kept tight control over every single detail of his clients' lives. They said you couldn't even sneeze without Joe Krupp knowing about it.

Angie glared at the stage door, which was now firmly closed. Krupp didn't know it, but he had just made her even more determined to get an interview with the boys from Zone.

JJ strutted along the edge of the stage, in tight, tight leather pants, his shirt unbuttoned to the waist, revealing a muscular, hairless chest, and a lean and gym-trained torso.

A hundred teenage girls in the first few rows squealed their approval. Few of them were over fourteen, even fewer of them had ever had a boyfriend, but every single one of them knew that JJ was without any doubt the sexiest thing that had ever taken to the stage.

JJ bent down, reaching out to touch their outstretched arms, and then pulled away suddenly, teasing them, exciting them, making them beg for more. He swayed his hips suggestively, and then spun around on his heels, turning to the other boys in the band. With the hand that wasn't holding his mike, he directed them, like the master-conductor of a world-famous orchestra.

Danny on drums, his face already drenched with sweat, grinned, and pounded out the beat, while Marco cut a mean riff on his electric guitar, and Luke went wild on the synthesizer.

But great-looking as the others were, all eyes were on JJ, as he turned back to his audience, and sang out the words to Zone's opening number, a raunchy rocker called "Are You Ready For It?" It seemed that he was born to sing the song, as he wrenched every ounce of emotion out of its lyrics and the audience screamed out their approval.

At the side of the stage, hidden from the audience, Krupp watched, with a satisfied smile on his face. This song was designed to whip the audience into a frenzy from the very start, and it was succeeding.

Zone were assured of a warm welcome in their

home town, he knew, but if JJ and the others could work this sort of magic on the nationwide tour he was already planning for them, then they could be the biggest thing in pop music within the next two years. And Joe Krupp would be richer by several million dollars.

JJ was undoubtedly the star of the show, and was revelling in all the adulation coming his way. It seemed that the more the audience screamed his name, the sexier he became.

He had them eating out of the palm of his hand, and, as he launched into the second number, a sharp-sounding tune called "Will You Be The One?", practically every member of the audience wished that she could indeed be the "One".

Towards the back of the hall, Rebecca, who was already clapping her hands and dancing in the aisle, turned to Angie. "Aren't they just great?" she asked, above the music and the screams of Zone's younger fans.

"They're OK," Angie said dismissively, even though her feet were betraying her feigned indifference by tapping along to the rhythm of the beat. "But take away their good looks, and JJ's dance routine, and what have you got?"

"Loosen up, Angie!" Rebecca chided her. "You're just being grumpy because you couldn't get backstage to interview them!"

Angie wagged an admonishing finger at her friend. "I'm not defeated yet, Bec Penswick," she said. "I promised to get an interview with them, and I'm not going to give up until I do!"

*   *   *

Angie sneaked around the back of the town hall, past the gaggle of adoring girls hanging around the stage door, to a tiny yard which backed on to the building. This was where the brewery van parked when it was delivering barrels of beer to the Town Hall bar.

Making sure that no one could see her, she bent down and tugged at the iron grating which she guessed led down to the cellars. Her plan was to get into the town hall via the cellar and, once inside, and out of the public area, she could try and track down Zone's dressing room, and get her prized interview with the boys.

Damn it! she cursed. The grating was too heavy and was barred from the inside. As she stood up she noticed a tiny window, set about thirteen feet up in the wall. She put her hands on her waist, grateful that she had the sort of slim physique which was the envy of most of the other girls at Astor College.

An empty beer barrel had been left in the yard, and she rolled that underneath the window. Standing on tiptoe, she reached up for the sill of the window and, with muscles aching painfully, hauled herself up to the open window.

It was a tight squeeze but she managed to get through, although not without ripping the legs of her jeans in the process. *Shoot! This interview had better be worth it!* she thought, as she clambered through and dropped carefully to the ground on the other side.

She was in some sort of store room. She crossed over to the door, thankful that it wasn't locked, and peered out into the corridor.

At the far end she could hear Krupp arguing with one of Zone's fans. No, he didn't care who she was, Angie heard him say, she couldn't have a quiet chat with his "boys". They would be signing autographs later and that would have to do.

This was Angie's chance, while Krupp and the bouncer were occupied. She ran down the corridor, in the direction of the stage, guessing that that was where the boys' dressing room would be.

She heard Krupp bid the fan goodbye, and march off down the corridor. Panicking, she opened the first door she came to: as luck would have it, it was the very room she had been searching for. Krupp's footsteps came echoing down the corridor. It was obvious that he was headed for the dressing room as well.

There was a large wardrobe in the corner of the room. Angie raced over and hid herself in it, huddling against the stage costumes belonging to the boys from Zone. Her heart pounding, she heard the door to the dressing room swing open. Krupp's footsteps marched across the stone floor. Coming right for her. The door to the wardrobe creaked open.

"Well, well, well, and what do we have here then?"

Angie breathed a sigh of relief. It wasn't Krupp! The manager had not been making for the dressing room after all. Instead, grinning at her, and obviously incredibly amused, was that handsome lead singer. He offered her his hand and she stepped out of the wardrobe.

"Thanks, EJ," she said.

"It's JJ, babe," he corrected her, and then turned to the other members of the band who were just filing into the dressing room. "Hey, gang, look what's just come out of the closet!"

The three others grinned; Luke even wolf-whistled. They then carried on as though nothing unusual had happened. Marco started stripping off, to get ready for his after-gig shower.

"And what are you doing here, babe?" JJ asked.

If he calls me babe again, I'll kill him! Angie thought.

"My name's Angie," she said. "Angie Markowska."

"That's an interesting name," JJ said.

"My dad was born in Warsaw," she explained. "I'm half Polish."

"The pretty half, of course."

JJ looked Angie appreciatively up and down, smiling that wicked little half-smile which he knew made him look really sexy. That smile was guaranteed to make his fans swoon in a second, and he frowned when Angie showed not the slightest sign of being impressed by it.

"So what do you want?" he asked again.

"I'm a journalist," she said, suddenly aware that her hair was a mess and her face was black and dirty from having climbed through the window, "for the local student newspaper."

"Aha!" said JJ smugly. "So you want to interview me, is that it?"

"Not just you, JJ," she said. "The others as well."

"What d'you say boys?" JJ asked. "Should we let this pretty young thing talk to us?"

Of all the patronizing, big-headed...!

The others shrugged. "It's up to you, JJ," said Danny, the cute young one. "As long as Joe doesn't find out."

"How did you get in here in the first place?" JJ asked Angie.

"Through a back window..."

JJ laughed. "That's crafty," he said. "I admire that."

"So you're quite willing to do an interview, JJ?" Angie asked, all business-like as she tried not to notice Marco's athletic body: he was crossing the dressing room on his way to the showers, dressed only in his white Calvin Kleins.

"Sure, why not?" said JJ. He sat down, and offered Angie a seat. He leaned back in his chair, and placed his leather-clad legs on the coffee table which was between him and Angie. She took the tiny tape-recorder out of her bag, and set it up on the table. "There's nothing I like better than pleasing the Press..." He chuckled, and winked over at Luke and Danny before turning back to Angie. "You did say you were a journalist, didn't you? You're a lot prettier than most of the *real* reporters I've seen..."

Angie glared angrily at him. She'd caught JJ's suggestion that she wasn't quite the professional lady of the press that she liked to think she was.

Resisting her natural urge to tell JJ just what she thought of him, Angie simply smiled sweetly and said: "I might not be working for Fleet Street or the BBC, JJ, even though I hope to one day, but let me remind you that I succeeded in getting past your manager's security, and the other members of the Press didn't."

Danny, the drummer, who had been listening in on the conversation, took a sip from his can of diet Coke, and laughed. "She's got you on that one, JJ," he said. "Not even the SAS can get past Joe when he's in a bad mood!"

"And what's more, JJ," Angie continued, still smiling, "it's perfectly true that I'm only working on a newspaper for unimportant schoolkids and college students. But just remember that it's those unimportant schoolkids and college students who are going to buy your records, and, if you're really lucky, make you rich and famous one day…"

She suddenly dropped her smile and fixed the handsome young singer with stern and reproving eyes. "Now, shall we get on with the interview?" she asked brusquely.

JJ looked strangely at Angie. No one had ever stood up to him like that before, especially not a girl as attractive as Angie. After all, he was the star of Zone, their lead singer and their songwriter. He was the one, Joe Krupp had promised, whose face was going to be in all the teen magazines within twelve months.

Hey, he needed a little respect! And then JJ realized that respect was exactly what Angie was demanding too.

She had spirit, this girl, JJ thought, and he found he liked that. He liked it very much indeed.

"OK, sure, let's get it over with," he said grumpily. Angie might have won the first round, but there were several more to go!

"Great!" Angie grinned, and switched on the tape recorder. "Now first question—"

JJ interrupted her and turned around to shoo Danny away. The young drummer had settled himself down in a nearby chair to listen to the interview.

"This is private, Dan!" JJ said jokingly. "I'm gonna tell –" he looked at Angie – "what did you say your name was again, babe?"

"Angie." *And don't call me babe!*

"Yeah, that's right, Angie," he said and turned back to Danny. "I'm gonna tell Angie all my deep and darkest secrets, and I don't want you or any of the boys to get to hear them, do I?"

Danny shrugged and stood up. "Sure," he chuckled, and walked away out of earshot. As he did so, and from behind JJ's back, he gave Angie an encouraging thumbs-up sign. Angie grinned: it seemed as though she had an ally in Danny already.

JJ turned back to Angie, and smiled sexily at her once more. Once again, it didn't make the slightest impression on her. What *did* make an impression on her, however, had been JJ's brief words to Danny. It had been interesting to see the lead singer drop his brash and self-assured mask for just a moment, and reveal the real JJ – who was genuinely embarrassed at having one of his mates listen in on his interview.

But when he looked at Angie again, he was the

50

cool rock star he played on stage once more.

"OK, let's roll, babe—"

"The name is Angie," she said sternly.

"Whoops, sorry, ba – Angie!" JJ teased. Angie found it impossible not to smile. She glanced down at her notes.

"What does JJ stand for?" she asked.

JJ held his hands up, palms facing Angie, in a mock gesture of defence. "Top secret," he replied. "Next question please!"

Angie glowered at JJ through narrowed eyes. If this second-rate pop star was going to answer all her questions in a similar manner she might as well go home now!

"OK, let's try something which you might be able to remember," she said patronizingly.

JJ grinned. Angie was treating him like a particularly irritating baby brother! She was sure a refreshing change from all those people who kept on telling him exactly how wonderful he was!

Angie asked him about how he and the others had got together in the first place and formed Zone. Marco had been studying classical music at a private school in the area, he told her, and Luke and Danny were fellow students in a stage school in Birmingham, although not in the same year. They'd formed a rock group and started playing the odd local gig.

"Then Joe Krupp came along," JJ said. "And he saw the guys' potential, and signed them up. But they lacked something, you know…"

"And what was that?" Angie asked and found

her eyes wandering from JJ's face, to his open shirt. A tiny crucifix hung from his neck, and nestled in the groove between his pectorals. The muscles were firm and well-defined, obvious evidence that JJ spent a lot of his free time in the gym.

"What were they lacking?" JJ asked, in a blasé fashion, and leaned even further back in his chair. "Good songs – anyone can play that top twenty trash: the public wants something different and original, you know. Plus they needed a dancer. And, of course, an impossibly handsome and sexy lead singer!"

"So I take it they're still searching for one, are they?" Angie asked sarcastically.

For a second JJ looked as though he was about to explode with indignation; and then he relaxed and grinned, realizing that not only had Angie won round one, but round two was hers as well!

"So Krupp found me," he continued. "I'd been a friend of Danny's from way back – I knew his sister, Eva..."

"Eva?" The Germanic name was an odd one for the sister of someone like Danny, whose family was obviously of Mediterranean origin.

"Yeah," JJ said. "Danny's mother was half-German – he speaks the language like a native. They named his sister after her maternal grandmother." JJ suddenly coloured, as though he was embarrassed about something. "Look, I thought we were supposed to be talking about me?" he said quickly.

"Sure. Go ahead, JJ," Angie said, interested, detecting a possible romantic angle for her story. She made a mental note to ask JJ about Danny's sister later.

"I got on well with the other guys," he continued, "I started writing their songs, organizing their dance routines, and that's how the best-looking pop band in the history of music came about!"

"And what about the mysterious JJ? Why do I get the feeling you're keeping something from me? Exactly where did Krupp find you?"

JJ leaned forward and reached out to switch off Angie's tape recorder. "I've got a better idea," he said huskily, and gazed into her blue eyes. "Why don't you tell me where *you're* coming from – like maybe over dinner tonight?"

Angie switched the tape recorder back on. "Sorry, I conduct interviews – I don't give them," she said smartly.

"You'll be sorry," he told her, trying to sound as if Angie's refusal hadn't disappointed him at all. "All my other girlfriends have had no complaints."

"They like hamburger and chips in a greasy spoon caff then, do they?" Angie asked patronizingly, and followed up JJ's remark with: "So, JJ, do you have a girlfriend at the moment?"

JJ smirked, and silently congratulated himself for managing to change the subject so successfully. *Round three to me, babe!* he thought. *You're not quite so on the ball as you like to think!*

JJ ran a nonchalant hand through his thick,

uncombed dark-blond hair, which, Angie noted, curled so cutely over the top of his shirt collar.

"Too much of a hassle, you know," he said, sounding like an experienced man of the world, although a quick glance at Zone's official biography would have revealed that he wasn't yet twenty-one. "You see a girl a couple of times and then the next thing you know she wants to go steady with you. Or she's only interested in you because she thinks you'll be famous one day." He shrugged philosophically. "Love 'em and leave 'em, that's my motto..."

You arrogant, self-opinionated chauvinist pig, Angie wanted to say. With his perfectly proportioned body, mischievous eyes, and that divine little dimple in the middle of his chin which she couldn't take her eyes off, Angie knew that JJ could have his pick of girls.

Yet she controlled her anger, because there was something about JJ's manner which jarred. Maybe it was the fact that he didn't look her in the eyes, when he spoke about his "girlfriends"; maybe it was his body language as he crossed and then uncrossed his legs; but something told Angie that JJ wasn't quite telling her the entire truth.

" 'Love 'em and leave 'em'," Angie repeated JJ's words, and watched as he shifted uncomfortably in his chair at the sound of his own words. "Can I quote you on that?"

"You will be quoting JJ on nothing," said a stern and familiar voice behind her.

Angie saw JJ's face fall, and she turned to see

Krupp standing behind her. Once again he had crept up silently on her, like a hungry puma stalking its prey.

"Er, hi, Mister Krupp," she said weakly, and stood up.

Krupp didn't return her welcome, but reached down and switched off Angie's tape recorder. He took the cassette out and put it into the pocket of his jacket.

"I believe I banned you from my boys' dressing room," Krupp said, grimly.

"Joe, she wasn't doing any harm," JJ pleaded on Angie's behalf. Angie thought she could detect a note of fear in his voice. "She was just interviewing me for her school paper, that's all."

Krupp shook his head sadly. "How many times must I tell you, JJ? There are to be no interviews until I decide the time is right," he said. He patted the pocket into which he had dropped Angie's cassette, as if to reassure himself that it was still there. "Trust me – I have only your best interests at heart. Have you ever known me let you down before?"

JJ hung his head. "No, Joe, of course not..."

Krupp smiled at JJ, and then turned his attention to Angie. He stopped smiling. "And as for you, young lady, you are guilty of breaking and entering. Perhaps I should inform the police..."

"No, Joe, you can't do that!" JJ cried, taking even Angie aback by the urgency in his voice.

Like he's frightened of something, she realized.

For a second JJ and Krupp stared at each other, as though engaged in a battle of wills. Finally

Krupp conceded defeat by averting his eyes, and took Angie's arm.

"You have a convincing defender in JJ," he said, and led her to the door. "But pull a stunt like this again and I shall have no hesitation in reporting the entire matter to the police!"

Angie just had the chance to nod her thanks to JJ before Krupp escorted her out of the dressing room, and slammed the door shut behind her.

Left alone in the room, JJ breathed out a sigh of relief. The door to the adjoining dressing room opened, and Luke, Danny and Marco came out.

"You sure lucked out on that one, didn't you?" Danny chuckled, and went over to give JJ a consoling pat on the back.

"Were you miserable scumballs eavesdropping at the door?" JJ asked, pretending to be shocked. Danny nodded happily.

"What's wrong, my man?" Marco, who was drying his hair after his shower, asked evilly. "The old JJ magic not workin' any more? I thought you could get any babe you wanted."

"She's not a babe," JJ corrected him, "her name's Angie…"

"So she's got a name," Luke said dismissively. "You still didn't get a date with her, SuperStud!"

Before JJ had joined the band, Luke had always been the one the fans swooned over, and now there was an element of not entirely friendly rivalry between the two of them.

"Leave it out, Luke," JJ said. "Angie's different. She's got brains, for one thing; and she's her own person. She stood up to me – no one else has done recently. She's not like all the others."

"I'll say that," agreed Marco. "She said no to you for one thing!" By Marco's side, Danny didn't say a word.

"It looks like you've lost your touch, JJ," Marco continued to tease. "Maybe we should think about getting us a new lead singer…"

"Let me tell you, Marco, my man, that JJ never loses his touch," JJ bragged, now that his chatting-up skills had been called into question. "If I'd really wanted her, I could have got her to agree to go on a date with me."

Luke looked his friend in the eye. "So prove it," he challenged.

"Prove it?" asked JJ, puzzled. "What d'you mean?"

"If you think you're such a gift to womankind, get this babe—"

"Angie," JJ corrected him.

"—get this Angie babe to agree to go out with you."

JJ shook his head. "Hey, I don't know that that's such a good idea," he said.

"What's wrong, JJ?" asked Marco, and mischievously added his own voice to Luke's challenge. "Think you're not up to it any more?"

"Yeah, JJ," Luke taunted, "what's the trouble? *Scared?*"

That did it. JJ took a step towards Luke.

"No one says that I'm scared," he snarled menacingly. "Not even you, Luke."

"Oh, yeah?" spat back Luke. "Well, I'm saying it."

"Cool down, guys," Danny said, coming between them. "Let's just forget about it, shall we?"

JJ shook his head. "No way am I going to forget it, Dan," he said. "I'll get a date with that babe."

Danny shook his head sadly. JJ's ego had been injured, and he wouldn't rest now until he had seen Angie again. Danny might have been three years younger than JJ, but he knew him much better than the other two guys in the band; and he knew that JJ felt a need always to prove himself. He also knew that if JJ went after Angie someone was bound to get hurt.

But who that "someone" was, Danny wasn't quite sure.

4

"**Y**ou're crazy, Angie!" Rebecca announced the following day, as she and Angie walked down the corridors leading to the office of the *Reporter*. There were only two days to go until Christmas, but the newspaper's office was still open.

Angie stopped, and made an exaggerated point of looking at her Swatch. "Congratulations, Bec," she said in a voice dripping with sarcasm.

Rebecca was puzzled. "Congratulations?" she said. "What for?"

"It's half-past eleven in the morning, and I picked you up from your Aunt Lizzy's house one and a half hours ago," Angie sniggered. "And it's taken you that long to tell me that I'm crazy!"

"I was practising phenomenal self-control," Rebecca explained without even a hint of sarcasm. "Adrian rang me up from his aunt's last night..."

"And how is he?" Angie asked.

Rebecca shuddered with pleasure. "Still as mind-numbingly gorgeous as ever," she said. "He

59

said he was sorry about the mix-up with the backstage pass…"

"That's sweet of him," Angie said. "He's a really considerate guy, Bec. Good-looking too."

"Yeah, I suppose he is," Rebecca said off-handedly, causing Angie to wonder if, despite all her words, her best friend might already be losing interest in her new boyfriend: after all they hadn't seen each other for almost forty-eight hours now, and for the love-struck Rebecca that was something of a record!

"He got a phone call last night," Rebecca went on. "From his cousin."

"From Luke?" Angie had only seen Zone's bass player briefly, and hadn't had the chance to tell him that she knew Adrian.

"That's right," Rebecca said. "He told Adrian everything about your interview with JJ last night after the concert."

"Yes, I was a bit of an idiot, wasn't I?" Angie admitted. "Letting their manager snatch that tape off me like that…"

"*Idiot?*" Rebecca couldn't believe what she was hearing. "Compared to you an amoeba has brains! Angie, you turned down a date with JJ himself!"

"Oh, yeah, I suppose I did…" Angie said calmly, secretly enjoying Rebecca's dismay.

"Is that all you can say, Angela Markowska?" Rebecca cried out. "There are thousands of girls out there who would die to have been in your position last night, and all you can say is 'Oh yeah'?"

"He's a good-looking guy, I'll give you that," Angie admitted, and remembered JJ's hazel-brown eyes, his shock of dark-blond hair, his teeth whiter than any she ever seen before... *And that divine little dimple right there in the middle of his chin.* "But he's an egomaniac. Thinks he's God's gift to women."

"And isn't he?" Rebecca definitely had her own views on that particular subject.

Angie ignored her, and started walking again. "He's found a little bit of fame, has a few lovestruck girls sending him adoring fan letters and hanging around the backstage door—" she continued.

"Like us, you mean," piped up Rebecca, until Angie silenced her with a threatening glare.

"—and he thinks he can call all the shots, and go out with whichever girl takes his fancy." They reached the *Reporter*'s office, and Angie started to open the door, still talking.

"Zone are still only a local band, Bec, remember that. They're nothing but a bunch of pretty boys who can vaguely sing in tune. They're a flash in the pan, and tomorrow no one will remember who they are. So if that arrogant, self-centred streak of ditchwater thinks he can turn my head by pretending to be some sort of great and famous rock star, then he's got another – Omigod, who's died?"

She had opened the door, only to be confronted by a newspaper office, the greyness of which usually bored Angie to tears, but which was now a vibrant shade of red, and whose normally stuffy atmosphere of printing ink and paper had been replaced by the sweet and heady fragrance of flowers.

Bouquets of red roses covered every available surface. There were scarlet blooms on Angie's own desk, even on the fax machine which had recently been given to the paper by a generous parent. The photocopier in the corner was piled high with bouquets too, as well as the bank of two Apple Macs which lined one wall.

In the middle of all the redness stood the tall, lanky figure of Steve, the eighteen-year-old editor of the school newspaper. He was holding in his hand a sealed envelope, and as soon as Angie entered the room, he handed it over to her.

"Yours, I believe? They arrived about an hour ago, by special delivery," he said in a sardonic voice, which suggested that he was not in the slightest bit amused by the fact that his office seemed to have been turned into a branch of the local florist's.

"All these roses are for me?" Angie asked incredulously as she tore open the envelope.

"Your name's on the envelope, isn't it?" Steve said. "At least I presume they're for you – you're the only Angie I know."

Rebecca peered over Angie's shoulder as she started to take the card out of its envelope.

"They're from Dominic Cairns, I know it!" she said definitely. Angie stopped in her tracks.

"Dominic Cairns? What do you mean?" she asked.

"Ever since you ran off from him at the

Christmas dance he's become obsessed with you!" Rebecca said. "He never talks about anything else!"

"Really?" Angie was suddenly very interested, so much so that she forgot about the envelope in her hands. "Dominic Cairns is obsessed with me?"

She remembered once again how much she had enjoyed dancing with Dominic a few nights ago: it had felt so good, and Dominic had been so kind and considerate even when she had suddenly run off and left him. He was so handsome too, with his curly, freshly-washed hair, and his dark Southern complexion. Any girl would be so lucky to go out with him.

Rebecca nodded furiously. "Well, come on!" she said impatiently. "Read his card!"

Angie smiled and took the card out of the envelope. "A hundred red roses from Dominic Cairns! It's quite a Christmas present, isn't it?" she said, as she turned the card over to read the message.

"Fifteen bouquets to be precise," came Steve's sarcastic comment as he tried to clear a space at his desk to work from.

"Wait a minute," said Rebecca. "It's December the twenty-third!"

"So what?" asked Steve.

"It's the middle of winter! Roses are out of season!"

Angie shook her head, as she read the message on the card. "Not in Australia," she sighed, and raised her eyes heavenwards. "These were flown in especially from Sydney last night."

"What!"

"Take a look at the card, Bec," Angie said and handed it to Rebecca. There was a delighted grin on Angie's face which she tried unsuccessfully to hide.

Rebecca's normally large eyes grew even bigger as she read the message on the card. She looked up at her best friend in amazement. "These are from JJ?" she gasped.

"That's what it says," Angie said, and took the card from Rebecca and read the message aloud: " 'To the best lady reporter there is. Sorry about the interview. Maybe we can hold it again over dinner. Thinking of you, JJ'."

"Angie, you have got it made!" Rebecca enthused. "JJ still wants to take you out to dinner!"

Angie picked up one of the bouquets and brought the flowers to her face. They smelt fresh and sweet. It had been a long time since anyone had bought her flowers, and roses had always been her favourites. It was a lovely idea of JJ's to apologize for last night: maybe he wasn't such a bad guy after all...

Angie Markowska, what are you thinking? she instantly scolded herself.

Angie replaced the card inside its envelope and casually tossed it on to her desk. "If I know him, dinner will probably be egg and chips at the local greasy spoon, and then a quick grope in the back of his car," she said dismissively. "The guy's got no style."

"Ten million red roses isn't style then?" Rebecca

asked, and smelled their fragrance.

"It's showing off," Angie replied, "and don't exaggerate. He's just proving that he's flash and has got a bit of money to throw around. A single red rose would have been much more effective. But not even that would have worked 'cause I'm not going out with him."

"You're not?" Rebecca asked in amazement. "The hunkiest guy in the world wants to take you out to dinner and you're turning him down?"

"That's right," Angie said. "Let him go out with one of his fans who can spend the whole evening telling him just how wonderful he is and gazing into those big hazel eyes of his…"

"Hazel eyes? I didn't know he had hazel eyes."

"They're just like the colour of autumn leaves, after the rain," she said, recalling JJ staring into her own eyes last night.

Rebecca nodded wisely; even on the picture cover of Zone's single she'd never noticed the colour of JJ's eyes. She exchanged a knowing look with Steve, who had finally cleared a space at his desk: it seemed that JJ had had more of an effect on Angie than even she realized!

"Guys like JJ are all talk," Angie continued. "And besides, we've got absolutely nothing in common."

"They do say that opposites attract," Rebecca said mischievously.

Angie paused for a moment, remembering what Stephanie had said about her feelings towards Angie's father. They were both so different, and yet Angie had never seen a happier couple.

Maybe away from the other members of the band, when he didn't feel a need to show off, JJ could be a different sort of person. She thought again of the way he had instantly sprung to her defence when Krupp had threatened to call in the police: that wasn't the action of a selfish, opinionated prig.

"Well, no way do these two opposites attract," Angie claimed stubbornly. "And no matter how many roses he sends me – he can send me the whole of Kew Gardens if he likes – I'm not going to let myself become the latest in his string of one-night stands!"

"You don't know he's like that!" Rebecca said, slightly put out that the integrity of her favourite singer was being brought into question.

"You know what they say about rock stars, don't you?" Angie said, echoing her stepmother's words.

"Yes," Rebecca said dreamily, hoping that at least half of what she'd heard about wild parties and fast living was true.

"And anyway, I've got much more important things to take care of," Angie said.

Rebecca groaned: she'd heard it all before. "I know: revision, articles for the *Recorder*, your work for the kids at Cuttleigh..."

Angie shook her head; there was a wicked twinkle in her blue eyes. "No – Dominic Cairns. Do you think he really does like me?"

5

"OK, Aunt Lizzie, you tell her she's mad as well!" Rebecca demanded and looked over at her aunt. Because her father was so often away on business, Rebecca usually stayed at the house of her aunt, an unconventional fiftysomething woman, who always dressed in long ethnic skirts, and wore long strings of brightly-coloured beads. A wealthy woman, she still looked as though her clothes had been bought from the local Oxfam shop, rather than from some of the trendiest modern designers, and her long greying hair refused any attempts to keep it kempt and tidy.

Angie groaned: Rebecca was beginning to sound like an old worn record now. Couldn't she get it into her head once and for all that she wasn't in the slightest bit interested in JJ and his macho posturing?

Aunt Lizzie peered at Angie through her glasses, as she poured the girls Earl Grey tea from a big china teapot.

"No, Rebecca, I don't think Angie's mad at all," she said. "Unlike certain people – " she darted a disapproving but playful look over at her niece – "Angie isn't just interested in how good-looking or sexy a boy is—"

Angie nodded: for an ageing hippy, Rebecca's Aunt Lizzie spoke far more sense than many other people her own age. She also had a spooky way of knowing exactly what you were feeling or thinking without you ever having to tell her.

"Angie could have her pick of the handsomest boys at that college of yours," Aunt Lizzie continued, and handed the embarrassed Angie a cup of steaming tea. "But I think that for her it's the person underneath that counts. It's not what a boy is that matters to Angie, but *who* he is. Isn't that right, my dear?"

Angie smiled: with the possible exception of Stephanie, Aunt Lizzie was the one grown-up she felt perfectly comfortable with talking about her private life. But whereas Angie always suspected that Stephanie would report back to her dad, she knew that all her secrets were safe with Aunt Lizzie.

"They've got to be more than hunks," Angie agreed. "Sure, JJ's cute and he's got a great body. You can tell that he probably works out at the gym every day. But looks aren't everything. A boy should be kind, and considerate, and gentle too."

"A woman needs to be treated like a lady," Aunt Lizzie said. She looked down as she fondly remembered her own late husband. "Not just as a trophy to be worn on some man's arm, like the latest trendy accessory."

"Exactly," Angie said, with feeling. "Like

Dominic Cairns – he's such a nice guy, even after I treated him so badly at the dance the other night. Thoughtful, charming…"

"And a major hunk too," Rebecca pointed out.

"That's an added bonus," giggled Angie, and then added, self-righteously: "But even if he was a spotty fourth-former I'd still like him."

"Oh, yeah?" Rebecca wasn't convinced; for that matter, neither was Angie.

Aunt Lizzie smiled, and offered them a plate of her home-baked muesli flapjacks. "Somehow I think that when Angie falls in love it will be for ever," she said, "and it will be as big a surprise to her as to anyone else!"

"Angie's too obsessed with her work, and getting a good job when she leaves college," Rebecca said. "She won't fall in love for years yet!"

"I wouldn't be so sure of that," said Aunt Lizzie, and peered at Angie over the rim of her teacup, in that creepy way she had when she knew something that no one else did. "I wouldn't be too sure of that at all…"

Angie stared at the phone, as if wondering whether she should go through with her plan, and then, for the third time that evening, started to dial the number. This time she didn't put the receiver down before the last digit, and she heard the ringing tone at the other end.

What's the big deal? she told herself. *This is the 1990s – a girl can ask a guy out for a date! Especially a guy who's obsessed with her! And*

Rebecca's right – maybe I do need a boyfriend.

There was a click at the other end as someone picked up the phone, and a dark-brown voice with a slight Scottish burr answered.

"Hello, Dominic, it's me, Angie," Angie breezed cheerfully.

On the other end of the line she could almost hear Dominic Cairns draw in his breath. It seemed like Rebecca was right again: Dominic really did like her a lot! She wondered why he'd never asked her to dance before, or invited her to the cinema or something. After all, they had known each other for several years now. Maybe he was just shy, although it seemed odd that someone as good-looking and as popular as Dominic Cairns could ever be unsure of himself.

"Hi, Angela," Dominic said. He sounded delighted to hear from her, and more than a little surprised. "It's nice to hear from you." There was just a touch of sarcasm in his voice, as if he hadn't really forgiven her yet for leaving him on the dance floor a few days ago.

"Look, Dominic, I'm really sorry about the other night," Angie said, determined to get the unpleasant part of her conversation out of the way first of all. "I was way out of order."

"No problem, Angela," Dominic said generously. "I understand – you had a story to get. Forget about it..."

"That's sweet, Dominic," she said. "But I'd like to make it up to you."

"Oh?"

"It's Christmas Eve tomorrow," she said. "And

70

Rebecca and Adrian are going out for a meal. So I was wondering if you'd like to come along too and make up a foursome – that is, if you're not doing anything..."

"No, I'm not doing anything," Dominic laughed, even though he'd promised to go to a party with the other members of the football team. He made a mental note to cancel.

"Then it's a date! Half-past seven on Christmas Eve!"

"Half-past seven it is," Dominic confirmed. "And Angela—"

"Yes?"

"I can't wait!"

Vito's was a trendy bistro much frequented by the local college students, and indeed anyone else who liked to think that they were in the slightest bit fashionable. Famed for the largest and tastiest pizzas and pasta dishes anywhere in town, it was always crowded by the early evening.

As it was Christmas Eve it was even busier than usual, and Vito had made sure that the restaurant was decorated in a suitably seasonal style. Red and green streamers and balloons decorated the room, and large sprigs of mistletoe hung over each table; awful Christmas muzak came over the sound system, although Vito thankfully kept it to the minimum.

Dominic leant back in his chair and patted his stomach. He had just demolished a huge bowl of fettucine. There was a healthy-looking glow on his face, the result of the three glasses of red wine he had drunk.

Angie gazed at him admiringly: he looked gorgeous in his linen jacket and shirt, and that lock of hair which kept flopping over his eyes made him even more irresistible. She had already noticed several attractive women glance in his direction, but the captain of the football team seemed to have eyes only for her.

Not that he had ignored Rebecca and Adrian, however. For the past hour and a half he had kept them all entertained with stories of some of the antics he and his fellow team-members got up to on their away matches.

He had cracked jokes which made them all split their sides with laughter, had listened sympathetically when Adrian had complained about the grades he was getting at the tech, and throughout the meal had ensured that everyone's wine glass was full.

Even so, his attention inevitably returned to Angie – or Angela as he persisted in calling her, making Angie feel important and ladylike – and Angie felt herself warming even more to Dominic. Dominic Cairns was charming, witty, and, if the tantalizing glimpse of his chest through his shirt didn't deceive her, possessed a body most girls would kill for.

He even had brains and breeding, as he'd demonstrated when ordering the wine for the meal: he'd surprised their snooty waiter by choosing an obscure-sounding wine which proved to be the most excellent bottle on the wine list.

Dominic was the sort of person any girl would be happy to go out with, Angie decided; smart, tidy and responsible, he was the sort of boy she'd even be proud to take home to her dad.

Unlike some other hunks, she thought.

Conversation inevitably got round to Angie's escapade the other night, when she had tried to gatecrash Zone's concert. Dominic was amused: Angie had shown the sort of ingenuity he could never have dreamed of.

"I'd never have the nerve to do what you did, Angela," he said, self-effacingly. "I'm proud of you."

"It was nothing," she said dismissively, although Dominic's compliment made her glow inside. "If I'm going to become a successful investigative reporter then that sort of thing is going to be all in the course of a day's work."

"I'm sorry that you lucked out in the end though," said Adrian, his arm draped over Rebecca's shoulder. "Do you want me to have a word with my cousin? Maybe he could wangle you another interview."

Angie shook her head firmly. "No way," she said. "After seeing Zone I'm not even convinced that they're going to be that big anyway. They're just another group of pretty boys with so-so voices and average songs."

Rebecca laughed. "And a lead singer who's madly in love with you!"

Angie glared at her best friend. "He was trying to chat me up like the little creep he is, that was all!" she protested. "Don't exaggerate!'

73

Dominic turned to Angie, a frown on his face. Angie had kept that part of her interview with Zone tactfully out of the conversation.

"JJ was coming on to you?" he asked, and Angie detected a note of jealousy in his voice, and a dangerous look in his eyes.

"It was nothing," she shrugged dismissively, and placed a reassuring hand on his. "And I'm not interested in him at all, if that's what's worrying you. We've got nothing in common with each other, for one thing."

Dominic smiled, and relaxed. "Good, then I'm pleased," he said, and was about to say something else when there was a commotion at the door of the restaurant. They all turned round to see what was happening.

"Well, well, well," said Rebecca, and shook her head in glad amazement. "Talk of the devil..."

JJ and the boys from Zone had arrived and were arguing with Vito at the reception desk. The smooth owner of the bistro was obviously finding fault with the way Zone were dressed. The bistro was by no means a formal restaurant, but Vito did require a certain smartness of appearance: it was obvious that he didn't think that JJ's leathers, Marco and Luke's scruffy jeans and MA flight-jackets, and Danny's back-to-front baseball cap quite came up to the sartorial standards he required of his guests.

Angie groaned, and hid her face behind her menu, hoping that JJ wouldn't catch sight of her. Despite herself, however, she found herself sneaking a glimpse over the top of the menu, and watched with the others as JJ pointed out to Vito that they did, in fact, have a reservation.

Vito, however, was insistent: they could not have a table dressed like that, booking or no booking. Things were starting to get a little ugly, when one of the waiters went up to Vito and whispered something in his boss's ear. Vito's expression changed instantly, and he beamed at the boys, shaking them each by the hand, and welcoming them warmly to his restaurant.

"Now, even I think that is gross," said Rebecca.

"What happened?" asked a puzzled Dominic. "Why's he changed his mind so abruptly?"

"I imagine someone's just told him that Zone are going to be famous one day, and might bring in more business for him," Angie said. "I can't understand how anyone can be so impressed with all that glamour and showbiz hype."

"It's OK for you to say that," said Rebecca. "Your dad works in TV – you're used to celebrities phoning him up, or taking him out..."

"I'd very much like to meet your father one day," Dominic cut in. "Everyone's seen him on those late-night arts programmes. He must be a very interesting man..."

Rebecca, who didn't take kindly to being interrupted, shot Dominic a silencing look. "As I was saying," she continued, "Angie's used to all this showbiz glamour. We common people have to snatch it when we can." She nudged Adrian. "Go on, Adrian, Luke's your cousin! Invite them to our table!"

"Bec!" Angie said, but it was too late: Adrian

had already stood up and waved Luke and the others over. The boys swaggered over to their table and Adrian introduced them to Rebecca and Dominic.

It was obvious that JJ didn't think much of Angie's dinner companion; he sneered at his smart and conventional clothes, and obvious good looks. Dominic, for his part, glared evilly at the young rock singer.

"And of course you remember Angie, don't you?" Adrian said.

JJ looked down at the blushing Angie, and smiled his sexy smile. "How could I ever forget her?" he said huskily.

Angie groaned inwardly: what a clichéd line. Even Danny chuckled at his best friend's studied and deliberate crassness.

"You got my roses, did you?" he asked.

"Yes, thank you," Angie replied frostily.

"So maybe you'd like to continue our interview over dinner?" he asked, and crouched down so as to be able to look Angie directly in the eyes.

Marco and Luke exchanged amused glances: JJ was working what he called his "seductometer" at full power. He must really want to win their challenge, they thought.

"And maybe Angela doesn't want to go out to dinner with you!" Dominic said roughly.

Angie looked sharply at him. "I can handle this myself," she said. She turned back to JJ. "JJ, if I get the urge for jelly and custard I'll give you a ring, OK? In the meantime, why not stop trying to be a big boy and go back to your playpen?"

"I guess that means no, then?" JJ asked, while behind him Danny, Luke and Mark sniggered.

"You've got it in one!"

JJ smiled philosophically, and stood up, but not before planting a quick kiss on Angie's cheek. Dominic pushed his chair back, and stood up angrily; the boys from Zone tensed, expecting trouble.

It was Angie who took hold of Dominic's hand, and made him sit down again: she didn't want anyone else fighting her battles for her. She glared angrily at JJ, who just grinned cheekily, and reached up for the sprig of mistletoe that was hanging over Angie's chair. He pulled it down and handed it to her.

Angie's anger turned to amusement, and she smiled too, as, without saying a word, JJ gave her a cute little wave, and swaggered off after the other members of the band to the choicest corner of the bistro where their table was waiting for them.

Angie touched her cheek. The spot where JJ had kissed it felt hot and tingling.

"Angela? Are you OK?" she was vaguely aware of Dominic asking her. "That was a lousy trick to play on you, wasn't it?"

"It's Christmas, Dominic," she said. "It's traditional."

Dominic draped a protective arm over Angie's shoulder. "He's a little creep," he decided, and watched as JJ sat down with the other guys. "And have you seen the way he dresses? Guys who dress in rags like that just show that they don't have any self-respect." With his free hand he self-consciously smoothed the creases of his smartly-cut linen jacket. Dominic knew he looked good in his designer clothes.

Angie followed Dominic's gaze. It was true that JJ and the other guys from Zone stuck out like a sore thumb in the bistro, but they also provided a sort of reverse glamour to the place.

While everyone else was drinking fine bottles of wine they had just ordered two pitchers of beer; and while everyone else had dressed up for their Christmas Eve meal JJ, Danny, Luke and Marco looked as if they had just tumbled out of a night club at half-past five in the morning. They added a sense of danger and excitement to Vito's stylish but normally laid-back bistro.

No one could take their eyes off the boys, with one surprising exception. Rebecca, of all people, was looking thoughtfully at her best friend, and when Angie turned back to ask her what she was staring at, Rebecca merely pointed to Angie's hands.

Without knowing it, she was still clutching fondly, and almost as if her life depended on it, JJ's sprig of mistletoe.

6

The following day – Christmas Day – was a quiet one for Angie, spent at home in front of the TV as it always was, with her father and Stephanie. Or rather it was spent mostly with Stephanie as her father had sequestered himself in his office, working on the scripts for a new TV programme he had been asked to direct. It was a six-part TV history of fashion in the twentieth century, and it was already being talked about excitedly in the newspapers. It was going to be a major TV series, they said, and it seemed that every famous designer in the world wanted his or her work featured on the show.

Even Angie had been impressed by the number of Christmas cards her dad had received this year. From Calvin Klein in Manhattan, through Gianni Versace in Milan, and even Issy Miyake in Tokyo, anyone who was anyone in the fashion world had sent the Markowskas their warmest Season's Greetings.

Angie idly wondered whether she could persuade her father to get her some cut-price designer clothes from his new-found friends, but realized what his answer would be. That was the trouble with having a dad with principles, she had laughingly complained to Stephanie as they sat in the big front room unwrapping their Christmas presents: you never got any perks.

Stephanie, who had also thought of asking her husband for the same favour before thinking better of it, agreed. She handed her stepdaughter a medium-sized parcel, wrapped in brightly-coloured paper.

"This was waiting for you on the doorstep this morning," she said.

"I didn't think the postman came on Christmas Day." Angie was puzzled.

"He doesn't," Stephanie said, and handed the packet over to Angie. "Someone must have dropped it off last night or early this morning."

Frowning, Angie tore the wrapping paper off the parcel to reveal a brightly-coloured box. She took off the lid, and peered inside. Another slightly smaller box was inside, and another, and another, like one of those Russian dolls her mum had brought back from St Petersburg where she had been dancing with the Kirov ballet.

Angie finally reached the last box. Inside was a plain unmarked envelope, and she tore it open.

Stephanie looked over her shoulder, by now just as fascinated as Angie was by what the envelope might contain. Angie held up a small cassette tape, and the two of them exchanged puzzled glances. Stephanie nodded over to the stereo system on the far wall.

"Play it," she suggested.

Angie went over and inserted the cassette into the tape deck and tapped the "play" button. She broke into a wide smile as her own voice and then JJ's came over the speakers.

"I don't believe it," she said, delightedly. "He got the tape of my interview back off Joe Krupp! That guy really is too much! Does he ever give up?"

Stephanie chuckled. "JJ must really like you if he defied the fearsome Krupp to help you," she said. "He's certainly determined, almost as much as you can be. Maybe you should take him up on his offer of dinner after all? It could be fun."

"No way," said Angie. She switched off the tape deck and took the cassette out. "After all, you know what they say about rock stars, don't you, Steph? And besides, I've got another date tomorrow afternoon…"

"You have?" Stephanie was immediately interested. There was nothing she liked better than a chat with her stepdaughter.

"He's called Dominic," said Angie, "and he's the kindest, sexiest and most charming guy I've met in a long, long time!"

"Wait a minute, can't you! I'm coming! I'm coming!" Rebecca's Aunt Lizzie called out, as she raced down the stairs to answer the insistent ringing on the doorbell.

Rebecca was still asleep. It was, after all, only half-past eleven: after dinner last night Rebecca and Adrian had gone off to a late-night club and

Rebecca had rolled in at four o'clock this morning – she thought she deserved a lie-in.

Lizzie, however, had been up since early morning, preparing the nut-roast that was to be their Christmas lunch. As usual she had several strings of beads round her neck and was dressed in a long flowing kaftan, but, as a concession to the season, she had tied a piece of bright-green tinsel around her waist.

She opened the door, and gazed appreciatively at the caller through her granny-glasses, looking him up and down, as she might inspect a prize piece of porcelain.

JJ was wearing his customary trendy black leathers, and the cheeks of his handsome face were rosy from the cold, and there were flecks of snow in his shock of dark-blond hair.

"Good morning, young man," she said pleasantly.

JJ shifted awkwardly from one foot to the other. "Er, good morning, ma'am," he began, but Lizzie interrupted him.

"Lizzie, my name is Lizzie," she told him, and pulled him inside. "Come into the warm, young man: it must be freezing out there!"

"Thanks, Lizzie," JJ said and smiled: there was something very endearing about Rebecca's aunt. Most women her age would have been put off by a leather-clad stranger turning up on the doorstep unannounced on Christmas morning; Lizzie, on the other hand, seemed ready to cluck and fuss over him like a mother hen over her brood. JJ liked her immediately.

"I suppose you've come to see Rebecca, haven't you?" Lizzie asked.

"As a matter of fact, yes, ma'am – I mean, Lizzie."

Aunt Lizzie let out a grand theatrical sigh. "Alas!" she smiled. "The handsome young gentlemen callers never come round calling for me!"

"Now that I really can't believe, Lizzie," JJ said, flirting good-naturedly with her. He accorded Lizzie a glimpse of his sexy half-smile which turned all the young girls wild. He was glad to see it had a similar effect on her.

Lizzie went to the foot of the stairs to rouse Rebecca, who called back that she would be down in a minute. While she waited, Lizzie turned back to JJ.

"I didn't catch your name?" she said.

"It's JJ, Lizzie."

"JJ." Lizzie repeated the name, savouring the sound. She recalled the conversation she had shared with Angie and Rebecca the other day, and realized who this handsome young stranger was. *So this is what pop stars look like these days*, she thought approvingly, remembering the long-haired, evil-looking rockers of her own youth.

"And what does JJ stand for, JJ?" she asked.

JJ grinned. "Sorry, Lizzie, top secret!"

Rebecca came down the stairs and gasped when she saw who had come to visit her on Christmas Day. She couldn't have been more surprised if it was Santa Claus himself. She instinctively wrapped her dressing gown more tightly around herself.

"JJ!" she breathed.

What were the other girls back at school going to say when they discovered that the great JJ from Zone had actually come around calling, at her house, at Rebecca Penswick's own house? She could hardly wait to get on the phone and tell them all.

"I don't understand," she started to babble, and ran a hand through her long blonde hair – *my God I must look like a real mess!* – "What are you doing here? How did you find out where I live?"

"Luke rang his cousin Adrian," JJ explained. "That's how I got the address."

"That wasn't very clever of Adrian," Aunt Lizzie tut-tutted. "I must have a word with that boy. He should know better than to give out Rebecca's address to all and sundry!"

Rebecca looked at her aunt as if she were mad. *This isn't All And Sundry, Aunt Lizzie,* she wanted to say. *This is a guy who's going to be one of the biggest and sexiest rock stars in the world one day soon. God bless you, Adrian!*

"You look tired," Rebecca remarked: there were dark rings under his eyes, and he looked like he hadn't slept in a long time. *Probably been raving all night long with some sexy girl in tow!* she assumed.

"Yeah, I was up all night, working on a song," he said and looked at his watch. "Listen, Rebecca, I haven't much time. Joe doesn't know I'm here and he'll kill me if he finds out. I know we've only just met, and you don't really know me, but I need a really big favour from you..."

As JJ told her what he wanted, Rebecca's face fell. For a second there, she had thought that JJ had come around to her house to ask her out. She should have known that that was too good to be true.

Still, what JJ was proposing did sound really exciting ... and so romantic that it even made up for the fact that she wasn't the focus of his attentions.

JJ turned to go, and Aunt Lizzie, with whom he had obviously scored something of a major hit, ushered him to the door.

"And the next time you do decide to visit, young man, telephone first," she said. She dived into the capacious pockets of her kaftan, and drew out a grubby and dog-eared business card which she pressed into JJ's hand.

After he had gone, Aunt Lizzie turned to her niece and waved her hand in front of her face as if trying to fan herself cool.

"What a hunk and a half!" she enthused, sounding more like a first-form schoolgirl than the kindly, if eccentric, old aunt she really was. "My dear, if only I was thirty years younger, the things I could show that young man...!"

Rebecca laughed. There were times when Aunt Lizzie acted and sounded like the most un-grown-up grown-up she had ever known.

JJ trudged through the snow, his collar turned up against the wind and the weather. His breath hung in icy clouds before him, as he walked to the posh restaurant where Joe Krupp was standing

Christmas dinner for JJ and the other guys from Zone.

There was an ulterior motive, of course: with Joe there always was. It seemed that the editor of one of the most popular teen magazines was up in town today, and at something of a loose end on Christmas Day of all days of the year. Joe had decided that this was the perfect time to treat the influential editor to a slap-up meal and some festive cheer while at the same time introducing JJ, Luke, Marco and Danny to him, and hopefully gaining some valuable press exposure for Zone.

It was the end of December, Krupp had announced to them a couple of days ago; in nine months' time, by the end of September, he wanted the name of Zone to be in every teenage music magazine in the country.

JJ wasn't bothered about impressing the music magazines, although he'd follow Joe's orders, coming on with the tough-guy act that Joe had decided was going to be JJ's image in the band. It wasn't really him, that wise-cracking, street-talking slicker, but Krupp assured him that that was what all the punters wanted these days.

What really mattered to JJ was the music, and he knew that whatever image Zone had, their music would still be successful. But Krupp had managed many other successful bands in his time, so he must know what he was talking about.

JJ's mind wasn't on the band's image, however: it was on Angie. What was it about that girl that was bugging him so? She was attractive, there was no doubt about that, although he'd seen more beautiful women. She was also very bright, something in a woman which always intrigued JJ.

Was it because he couldn't have her? That she hadn't been impressed by his good looks, and glamour, and the fame which everyone said was going to be his someday soon?

JJ could have had any girl he wanted – he only had to look outside the stage door at any local venue Zone were playing – but Angie was the only one to have turned him down. The only one, too, who didn't gawp at him with lovestruck eyes the minute he opened his mouth; the only one as strong-willed as he was. Hell, she wasn't doing his ego any favours, and that's why he'd accepted the gang's challenge to take her out on a date.

But he remembered how he felt last night when he saw Angie and Dominic together. The guy was a geek, pure and simple, JJ had decided, no matter how good-looking he might be.

With his well-cut and smart clothes, he was the complete opposite of JJ. How could Angie let someone as "solid" and "dependable" as Dominic take her out, let him put his arm on her shoulder? She was wasting herself on him.

She'd said she wanted to be a reporter: if she hung around with Dominic he knew that she might as well kiss goodbye to all those dreams. All Dominic would want would be a wife to wait for him to come home at the end of the day, practically handing him his slippers and telling him that his dinner was ready and waiting for him on the table.

Angie, he guessed, was determined to rise to the top in her chosen career, as determined as JJ was to do the same in his. He had seen that steely sense of purpose in her eyes, that same look that Danny and the others said was in his. He'd hate to see that dream shattered.

But there was something strange about Dominic too, JJ realized, something not quite right, something he couldn't put his finger on. Maybe it was the way he looked at Angie, hanging on to her every word, like JJ's fans did to him. Maybe it was the way Dominic never contradicted her, the way he always seemed to want to please her, always to say the things he knew Angie wanted to hear.

Dominic wanted to please Angie too much, JJ realized. No, it was something more than that: Dominic was *desperate* to please Angie...

Loosen up, man! he told himself. *You want what you can't have and that's what's screwing you about! That's all it is – pure and simple!*

Somehow, JJ didn't quite believe himself.

7

Angie gazed out in wonder at the field of snow before her. It was as if the entire countryside had been clothed in a sheet of white, interrupted only here and there by the black and spidery silhouettes of the bare winter trees, and the low and rough stone walls, which meandered their way across this part of the countryside. A few birds flew in the sky which was cloudless, a brilliant frosty blue, and the bright winter sun shining down made the ice and the snow sparkle and glisten even more.

She turned round to Dominic, who was sitting next to her on one of the stone walls. "It's beautiful, Dominic," she said. "So calm and peaceful."

Dominic smiled and nodded. "I know. I come out here a lot when I need to get away from the hustle and bustle of life back at college. It helps me to reflect, get things into perspective."

Angie laughed. "You're certainly not what I expected, Dominic Cairns," she admitted and moved nearer to him for warmth. They were both wearing their warmest leather jackets, and the wind had dropped, but it was still bitingly cold.

Dominic smiled, and turned to look at Angie. She saw that his dark hair had once again flopped into his eyes, and noticed that it was covered with snowflakes. "What do you mean, 'not what I expected'?" he asked in all seriousness.

"Well, when the captain of the football team asks you to go out with him for the afternoon, a girl expects to be forced to spend most of the day standing in a muddy field watching his grotty mates kick an old ball around," she joked. "She doesn't expect to be taken in his car—"

"In his dad's *borrowed* car," Dominic corrected her.

"OK. She doesn't expect to be taken in his dad's borrowed car, deep into the countryside, for a wonderful Boxing Day lunch. And then, after lunch, to walk to one of the most romantic spots for miles around," she said, and then added: "I think it's lovely, Dominic; it's a very pleasant surprise."

He put an arm over her shoulder, and cuddled her closer to him. "You're sure now, aren't you?" he asked. "I want today to be really special for you, Angela."

There was a strange urgent tone in his voice, which Angie put down to his desperately wanting to please her: *what a guy!* she thought happily.

"It's the best day of the year for me, Dominic," she said, and reached up to kiss him on the cheek. "And as it's December the twenty-sixth,

I've almost three hundred and sixty-five to choose from."

"You should never judge a book by its cover," Dominic laughed. "Appearances often deceive. You thought the captain of the football team could never be romantic. And you were wrong!"

Angie wagged an admonishing finger in his direction. "Aha, but you're not just the captain of the football team. You do know what they call you around the college, don't you?"

Dominic chuckled. "No. What do they call me?" he asked, although he knew only too well what his nickname was amongst the female students.

"Dishy Dominic!" Angie replied. "Dominic Dreamboat!"

"I'm flattered," he said, laughing off the compliment. "They must all have white sticks and guide dogs," he added self-deprecatingly.

Angie punched him playfully in the ribs. *Modest too!* she thought. *Unlike that rock 'n' roll creep with the divine dimple in the centre of his chin who thinks he's God's gift to women! Was Dominic anything but perfect?*

"Seriously, you're the best-looking guy in school," she told him.

It was something she would never have admitted to him before, fearing that it would make him even more big-headed than she had always assumed anyone that handsome already was. But now that she had got to know him, now that she had seen just how modest and unassuming he really was, she felt that she ought at least to tell him the truth.

"Are the rumours true – that you'd like to try and become a fashion model after you leave Astor College?"

Dominic shrugged a little self-consciously, as though his modelling ambitions embarrassed him a little, and that working as a model was certainly not the sort of career any level-headed, macho captain of a football team should even contemplate following.

"I'd like to," he finally admitted. "There's a lot of money to be made at the top in that business. But it's a tough, back-stabbing world and I really don't know if I've got what it takes..."

Angie looked at Dominic, from his brilliantly blue eyes, classic profile and Mediterranean complexion, across his broad and powerful shoulders, down his body, which, even though it was clad in a Schott leather jacket, clearly rippled with muscle, down every single inch of his six-foot-four height.

"Believe me, Dominic," she said. "You have most definitely got what it takes..."

Dominic smiled, with those perfectly white teeth of his, and pulled Angie closer to him. She didn't resist, but instead melted into his warm and welcoming arms, as though it was the most natural thing in the world.

They kissed, a tentative enquiring kiss at first, as though Dominic wasn't quite sure how far Angie would allow him to go. Dominic's full and soft lips felt like velvet, and tasted of the fine red wine he had had with his meal. His breath was fresh and warm. His strong hands cradled

Angie's head, and he stroked her hair, as tenderly as he would that of a small child or animal. Pulling her hair gently back, he traced the outline of her ears.

They separated, and smiled at each other. Each of their faces was flushed and red, although certainly not from the cold. Indeed, both Angie and Dominic were warmer than anyone should naturally have been in such weather.

Dominic beamed; his hair was mussed, and, despite his efforts, that wayward lock of hair had fallen once again over his eyes, making him look even more devastatingly desirable.

He raised a hand to her face, and with his fingers outlined the contours of her lips. This time it was Angie who reached out and drew him to her, pressing him next to her, enjoying the touch of another body alongside hers, of a strong male body.

She kissed him again, a fuller deeper kiss this time, and wrapped her arms around him, hugging him close to her, tightly as if she feared that he might vanish from her for ever.

Dominic grinned, and massaged the small of Angie's back. Even through the leather of her jacket his touch was like fire.

It felt so good to be with a boy again, Angie thought, so good to know there was someone who was attracted to you as much as you were to him.

It somehow made your life complete: your days could be as busy and as active as possible, but without a boy who loved you, without this confirmation and reassurance of your own worth, then they were as bleak and as unfruitful as the winter landscape Dominic had brought her to.

She drew back and smiled dreamily. "There," she breathed, "I hope that makes up for my leaving you at the Christmas dance a few nights ago."

Dominic grinned. "More than enough," he said gratefully. "I must admit I was a little disappointed when you ran off like that, after I'd been secretly plucking up the courage to ask you out for months."

For months?

This was news to Angie. Even Rebecca, who normally could spot the love-light in someone's eyes before anyone else, would have been surprised.

Dominic chuckled with embarrassment and for a second turned away from Angie, so as not to look her in the eye. "I guess I was ... kinda shy," he said.

The captain of the school football team, shy? The guy who, they all said, ruled his team with a rod of iron, and had turned them into one of the most successful teams in the local college soccer league – this guy was afraid to go up to a girl and ask her for a date? Angie couldn't believe that. However, she didn't pursue the matter.

"You had a right to be upset," she admitted frankly. "It was really bad-mannered of me. If that had happened to me I would have been furious."

Dominic shook his head. "Funnily enough I admired and respected you all the more for it," he said. "You're determined, and you'll do anything which is necessary to become a top journalist." He sighed. "I only wish I had your drive..."

Angie reached out and stroked his cheek; it was only late afternoon but already there were traces of stubble growing there. She liked that, liked the rough touch of his beard as she kissed him.

For some reason she found herself comparing him to JJ: JJ's pale skin was soft and smooth, and, even though he was a couple of years older than Dominic, she doubted whether he shaved more than once every two days. She supposed that that was what all those pre-pubescent schoolgirl fans like these days. *Let them keep their pretty boys,* Angie thought. *I want a real man like Dominic.*

"I'm sure you'll make it as a model one day, Dominic," she said encouragingly. "After all, you've definitely got the looks..."

Dominic looked doubtful. "Sometimes I'm not so sure," he admitted. "I've sent pictures of myself to all the main agencies, even a couple of the top magazines, but none of them ever bothers to reply..."

"It's the same in journalism," Angie said sympathetically. "If you don't know anyone it's that much harder to get a job..." A sudden thought struck her. "Say, why don't I ask my dad?"

"Your dad?"

"He's setting up this major TV programme about the history of fashion in the twentieth century," she said. "He's been in contact with all the top fashion designers."

"That's right," Dominic said slowly. "I remember reading something about it in one of the newspapers ... I never realized your dad was involved..."

"Well, maybe Dad can help you get your photographs seen by the people who really matter," Angie said excitedly.

"You really think so?" Dominic asked.

"It's worth a try, isn't it?"

Dominic took Angie's hands in his. "Angie, I don't know how I can ever begin to thank you," he said.

"I'm sure I'll think of something," she replied, and kissed him on the lips again. "You could help me out in a couple of days' time, on New Year's Eve, for starters."

Dominic frowned. "New Year's Eve? What's happening then?"

"I'm helping to organize a party for the children at Cuttleigh Hall – you know, the centre for disabled kids," she said. "With Government cuts it's the only bit of fun they get every year, poor things."

Dominic's face fell. "I'm really sorry, Angie," he said, sounding like he meant it. "I can't..."

"Is there something wrong?" Angie asked, trying to understand. "Lots of people feel uncomfortable in hospitals or around disabled kids..."

Dominic shook his head. "It's not that," he said. "Disabled kids are just as good as you or me – why should you feel uncomfortable around them? But ... but ... but I promised my parents that I'd go and see my grandmother that day. She's not very well, and it might be my last opportunity to see her."

"That's OK," Angie said, a trifle disappointed. It would have been so good to have taken Dominic along to Cuttleigh Hall, to show him off to her friends there.

"You know I'd really like to help you," Dominic continued, and added: "Especially as you're going to talk to your dad about me…"

"It doesn't matter, Dominic, believe me," she lied, and then held him close again.

She was the luckiest girl in the whole world, she decided. They were made for each other, that seemed certain, and Angie – and certainly Dominic – couldn't believe their good luck.

8

Cuttleigh Hall was a small children's day centre on the outskirts of town, and Angie had been working there on a part-time basis for almost three years now, in fact ever since she had decided that she wanted to become a journalist.

Originally, she had thought that a spot of charity work would look good on her CV, when she started on the dreaded round of job interviews; but, as the months progressed, and as she got to know the staff and children better, she found that she was enjoying her work enormously.

It's typical, she often sharply rebuked herself; I start doing something on a purely "business" level, and I end up getting personally involved!

Most of the children at Cuttleigh were mentally or physically handicapped, but the biggest handicap they all shared was other people's prejudices. Even Rebecca was guilty of this, and while Angie could understand her discomfort, she also knew that it was totally groundless. It was such a welcome relief to find people who treated disabled people just the same as everyone else. She smiled, as she remembered Dominic's words earlier that afternoon: "They're just as good as you or me." What a great, understanding and caring guy he was!

A few days after Christmas, Angie had had to leave Dominic to go to Cuttleigh, for an appointment with Nurse Clare, the director of the home. No longer a nurse, Nurse Clare was now a successful businesswoman and stalwart of the local community, but she still liked to refer to herself as one. Nurse Clare was a stout and tough seventy-year-old Scot who had run Cuttleigh for the past thirty years. She may have been formidable to look at in her tweeds, short cropped hair, sensible brogues and stern tortoise-shell glasses, but she had a heart of gold, and a highly-tuned sense of humour.

"After all," she would often say, "with the National Health Service receiving less and less money every year, and with my staff obliged to work more and more hours, you'd better have a sense of humour or you'd simply go bonkers!"

Angie had brought a file full of correspondence with her. Nurse Clare sifted through it, and congratulated her. "I don't know how we could manage without you," she said, approvingly. "You've done a sterling job, simply first-rate!"

Angie nodded her thanks. "I've arranged for the caterers to come in at noon on New Year's Eve – jelly, cakes, ice cream, the works!"

"And the entertainment?"

"A conjurer," Angie said, "and one of the very best. I actually got my dad to open his Filofax and pull a few strings for me – for once! The kids will love him!"

Nurse Clare chuckled, and leaned back in her chair, folding her arms and resting them on her ample bosom. "You're a blessed treasure, my poppet!" she said. "The best volunteer we've had since—" she waved her hand vaguely in the air "—since I don't know when. Since Jeremy certainly."

"Jeremy?"

Nurse Clare stroked her chin thoughtfully. "Jeremy? Or perhaps it was Henry? Or Merriman? I can never remember these boys' names. Most of 'em come and go so quickly. No staying power, boys!"

She shook her head dismissively: she was getting on a bit now, she realized, and at her age couldn't be expected to remember everyone's name.

"But whatever his name was, he was a godsend, exactly like you are, my dear. He worked here a few years ago, until he moved out of town."

She started to gather up all the papers Angie had brought in.

"We're all so grateful for all the work you've put in this year, Angie," she said. "It's reassuring to know that there are still people who care about others. All the other lasses your age seem to care about are the latest crooners in the Hit Parade—"

"The charts," Angie corrected her, "and we call them rock stars now." Nurse Clare might have to deal with the horrors of late 1990s Government bureaucracy but some of her vocabulary belonged to an entirely different age!

"—and their beaux," Nurse Clare continued, and then, in response to Angie's look of amusement, added, "Their boyfriends, I mean."

Angie turned shyly away from Nurse Clare. "Well, I might have a boyfriend, now..." she said.

"Really?" There was a note of disappointment in Nurse Clare's voice, as she wondered whether this would mean that Angie would be leaving Cuttleigh.

"You needn't worry, Nurse Clare," Angie reassured her. "Dominic's a wonderful guy, and I'm sure he won't mind me giving up a couple of evenings a week to work here. In fact, he's so wonderful he might actually come over and help me!"

"We shall see, my dear," Nurse Clare said quietly. "We shall see..."

"So has dishy Dominic asked you to go steady yet?" Rebecca demanded the following afternoon when she called round at Angie's for a chat and a slice of Stephanie's cheesecake.

"Bec! Don't you think of anything else?" Angie laughed, while over by the breakfast bar in the kitchen, Stephanie stifled a giggle behind her research papers.

"No: what else is there to think about?" was Rebecca's happy reply. "You really are the luckiest girl in the whole of the school, nabbing Dominic Dreamboat like that. Did he take you for a really romantic walk the other day in the snow?"

"As a matter of fact, he did," Angie said.

It felt wonderful discussing Dominic with Rebecca, who obviously thought she was in at the very beginning of the greatest romance Astor College had ever known.

Secret romances were all very well, Rebecca had once told her best friend, but they couldn't even begin to compare with the joy you felt when you realized that the whole world knew that someone loved you.

"He seems a really nice boy, from what Angie's told me," Stephanie said. "Responsible and well-mannered, from a good family. I'd like to meet him sometime soon, Angie."

"You will, Steph, you will," her stepdaughter promised, and joked: "But just remember you're married to Dad and that dishy Dominic's all mine!"

She turned back to Rebecca and asked her why she had come round: wasn't she supposed to be seeing Adrian today?

"Yeah," Rebecca said, and toyed with her cheesecake. "But I saw him over most of Christmas. I just fancied seeing you."

"Ah." Angie nodded wisely.

After Rebecca's confident announcement that Adrian was the only boy for her, it looked as though their passion was cooling off more quickly than the weather outside. Angie had seen it happen time and time again: Rebecca was always infatuated with one boy or another, but she bored of them easily, and rarely did her interest in them blossom into love.

Now Dominic and me, we're different … Angie found herself thinking.

"So where's Adrian, now that you've stood him up?" she asked her friend.

"I did not stand him up!" Rebecca protested. "I cancelled our date a good half-hour before we were due to meet up." She sliced two more portions of cheesecake, one for her and one for Angie. "He said it was OK and he'd give Luke a ring and see what the boys were doing…"

"He's gone out with JJ and the others?" Angie asked.

"He's gone out with Zone," Rebecca corrected her, "not 'JJ and the others'." There was a sly look in her eyes, and she picked up her plate of cheesecake and headed for the door.

"C'mon," she said, "let's listen to some music…"

Angie stood up to follow Rebecca when the outside door opened, and her father came in. He threw his leather-bound Filofax down onto the breakfast bar, and shuffled out of his snow-covered overcoat. Stephanie took it, and hung it up.

"Bad day at work, Mr Markowska?" Rebecca asked sympathetically. Angie's father was an even bigger workaholic than his daughter, and had been working at the TV centre all over the holiday, apart from Christmas Day itself, when he had been working from home.

Peter nodded, and kissed Angie on the cheek in welcome. Angie looked up adoringly into her dad's eyes, and Peter sighed: whenever Angie acted like this he knew she wanted something.

"Dad, I have a really huge favour to ask you," she said.

"I guessed," he said sarcastically.

"You know I went out with Dominic Cairns yesterday…"

"Stephanie told me last night," Mr Markowska said. "I know his father – he's a member of my club. Dominic seems a really nice lad. A great footballer too, by all accounts."

"Well, then you must know how good-looking he is and he wants to do some modelling work but he's not getting any positive responses from any of the agencies," Angie said, without pausing for breath. "And since you're working on this big fashion series, I thought, maybe—"

"No, Angie," Peter said firmly. "If he wants to succeed in this life he's going to have to do it on his own. I won't pull any strings to help you get a job in journalism and I am certainly not going to pull any strings for him."

"He sounds like such a nice boy, dear, solid and dependable," Stephanie said as she returned from hanging up her husband's coat. "Surely it wouldn't do any harm?" She winked at her stepdaughter. "And it would make Angie so happy."

Peter shook his head, and raised a hand to signal an end to the conversation. "Those contacts contained in there –" he pointed to his Filofax on the breakfast bar "– are privileged information. I'm sorry, Angie, if you want to be a journalist, or if your new boyfriend wants to become a top model, you can just go out there and do it yourselves. I am certainly not going to help you!"

"He's as stubborn as a mule!" Angie fumed, after she had stalked out of the kitchen into the lounge, followed by Rebecca. "He won't lift a finger to help either me or Dominic!"

"Chill out, Angie," Rebecca advised her, and took a cassette out of her bag, and slipped it into the tape deck. "You'll just have to tell Dominic the bad news. He'll be disappointed, but it won't break his heart."

"I'm not seeing him tonight," Angie said. "He's in training. Apparently there's a big match in a few days' time."

"A football widow already..." Rebecca joked, and switched on the cassette.

"Dominic's taking me out to dinner tomorrow night though," Angie revealed. "To Vincente's."

"Vincente's?" Rebecca was impressed. Vincente's was a top-rated swanky restaurant which, so they said, was the classiest place to eat this side of the Channel Tunnel. The service was impeccable, the food faultless, and the candle-lit tables in tiny alcoves the perfect places for romantic dinners *à deux*. The bill could also run into three figures. "I wish Adrian would take me somewhere like that! Dominic must like you one hell of a lot."

"He does," Angie agreed, "and I like him too. He's so gentle and caring and – what on Earth is that?"

She had just become aware of the music which was coming from Rebecca's cassette. It was a rough cut, obviously done not in a professional recording studio, but in someone's hotel room.

The song was a cheeky, slightly up-tempo piece, technically not particularly brilliant, and it was sung to the backing of a solitary acoustic guitar. And the voice singing it was deep, and soulful – and very, very familiar.

"I don't believe the cheek of him!" Angie gasped, but she couldn't stop the corners of her lips from creasing up into a smile.

"Sssh!" Rebecca urged. "Listen!"

As she listened to JJ's song, Angie's smile became even wider until it filled her entire face.

There is heaven in her eyes
  And heaven in her mind
Even in the way she looks
  And heaven in her smile.

Heaven's where she's been
  I'll need her till I die
I'm lonely when she's not there
  I'm haunted by her eyes.

There is heaven when she moves
  Like a phantom in the night
I reach out for her when I'm alone
  I know our love is right.

I guess I'm just a fool
  For the woman I can't win
But a girl who stands aloof from love
  Commits a deadly sin.

106

Words cannot describe
  What Angie means to me
And if she doesn't call me soon
  I swear that I will die...

"What is he *like*?" Angie marvelled. "Won't he ever take no for an answer?"

"Apparently not," Rebecca laughed. She'd been tempted to play the cassette JJ had given her when he had visited her on Christmas Day, but the look on Angie's face made the waiting worthwhile. "So why not go out with him, Angie?" she asked. "After he's tried so hard?"

"He's arrogant, self-opinionated and—"

"No, he's not," Rebecca cut in. "When he gave me that tape he said—"

"And you're just as bad helping him out, Bec!" Angie snapped, although there was no doubt that JJ's song had appealed both to her ego and to her sense of humour.

This creep of a guy had filled her office with roses. And now he had written a song for her. No one had ever done that: after all, it wasn't the sort of soppy thing you expected.

Well, not from people like Dominic, and Adrian, and all the other boys at Astor College.

"When he gave me that tape on Christmas morning," Rebecca continued, "I got the feeling that he really wanted to get to know you. That he was really sincere and genuine..."

"Him? He's about as sincere and genuine as a black widow spider," Angie said flippantly. "The difference is that a black widow spider is prettier."

"Oh, yeah?" said Rebecca.

Angie wasn't pulling the wool over her eyes. Who was it who had said that JJ's eyes were the colour of autumn leaves after the rain?

Who had presumed that JJ spent lots of his time in the gym, because she had noticed his crucifix nestling between his well-developed pectorals?

And who was it who couldn't get that cute little dimple of his out of her mind? Rebecca guessed that Angie was a lot more attracted to JJ than she liked to admit.

"Besides," Rebecca continued, "Aunt Lizzie liked him – and that's good enough for me!"

Angie paused for a moment, and thought. There were those of Rebecca's friends who said that Rebecca's Aunt Lizzie was psychic. Certainly with her long kaftans, the joss sticks which she used to perfume the bathroom, and her unconventional and "hippy" ways, Lizzie didn't do anything to discourage people from believing that she was an excellent judge of character.

There had been times when Angie had gone to Lizzie for advice. Sometimes it was advice on the suitability of a particular boyfriend, sometimes it was advice of a more personal nature which she would have been too embarrassed to ask her parents for.

But whatever words of wisdom Aunt Lizzie had given out, they had always been spot-on. Maybe she was right: maybe, away from the other guys in Zone, when he didn't have to show off and prove his worth as their lead singer and song-writer, maybe JJ was an OK guy after all.

Angie Markowska! she immediately scolded herself. *What do you think you're talking about? Are you out of your head, or what?*

"Sorry, Bec," she smiled. "I know you've wanted me and JJ to get together ever since I first interviewed him, but I'm seeing Dominic now. Nothing will ever get me to go out for dinner with JJ!"

Rebecca sighed philosophically. "I still think you're wrong," she said. "And Dominic need never know. But, with you out of the picture, I guess that means that we other girls might just be in with a chance!"

"What about Adrian?" Angie asked.

"Oh, yeah, I was forgetting about him..."

Angie was tut-tutting theatrically – Bec was quite simply impossible! – when the telephone rang. Rebecca, who had the ability to make herself at home in anyone's house, answered it. She passed the receiver over to Angie, who mouthed the words, "Who is it?"

"Don't worry, it's not JJ, not this time anyway," Rebecca sniggered. "It's Nurse Clare, from Cuttleigh. She says it's urgent."

Angie put the receiver to her ear, and frowned as she listened to what Nurse Clare had to say. After five minutes, she replaced the receiver and glanced over at Rebecca. There was a resigned and distinctly unhappy look on Angie's face.

"Bad news, huh?" Rebecca asked sympathetically. Angie nodded.

"The worst," she confirmed, and breathed a long theatrical sigh. "It looks like I'm going to have to take up JJ's offer of dinner after all!"

9

The car pulled up outside Angie's house at half-past seven on the dot. Even in the affluent neighbourhood in which she lived, where every second house belonged to someone working in one of the trendy professions, a top-of-the-range limousine gliding up to the kerb was still quite unusual. Add to that the fact that it was being driven by a hired chauffeur, dressed in a smart burgundy uniform and cap, and it was hardly surprising that, when Angie came to the door, thirteen net curtains twitched in thirteen different living rooms.

Angie felt like a queen, as she opened the door. She was dressed in a long, silken white dress, and a black satin waistcoat, the cut of which made her waist seem even smaller than it already was. A beautiful silver chain – understated but definitely classic – hung around her neck, and her hair was glossy and sleek.

A pair of diamond studs sparkled in her ears, glittering in the light from the overhead street-lamps which lined her avenue. Stephanie had loaned them to her especially for the night; or rather she would have done, if she had been around to lend them. Her dad and her stepmother had driven out of town to discuss with a top executive over a meal Peter's plans for his fashion show. They had no idea where Angie was going tonight – or who she was going with.

She looked a million dollars, and when Rebecca had asked her why she had gone to all this trouble for JJ, Angie had simply replied that JJ had told her he was taking her to his favourite restaurant in the whole of the country. It was very exclusive, he had warned her, and the proprietor wouldn't serve just everyone.

When Angie had pointedly and deliberately let slip the fact that Dominic was taking her to Vincente's the following night, JJ had just laughed and told her that, compared to the place he was taking her, Vincente's might as well just be an old greasy spoon caff stuck in the middle of nowhere.

His restaurant was real swish, he had said, so she'd better dress up like she was going to meet a member of the Royal Family. Or maybe someone even classier, as there was a rumour (and Angie wasn't quite sure if he was joking or not) that this joint was so stylish that one member of that particular family had already been turned away for being improperly dressed.

"And besides," Angie had told Rebecca, "I want to show JJ the sort of class act he's dealing with. What's he going to be dressed in? An off-the-peg suit and scruffy tennis shoes like every other third-rate rock star?"

She couldn't have been more wrong. When she opened the door she gasped at the sight – no, the *vision* before her.

JJ was dressed in a stylish, black frockcoat, its inside lined with red satin, and with a tiny red ribbon attached to its dark velvet lapels. Instead of his customary leathers, he wore black Tartar trousers, tucked into knee-length Russian boots, which had been shined so much that, if she had wanted to, she could have seen her face reflected in them.

He wore a linen, collarless, white shirt, and, in place of a traditional tie, a green velvet cravat with a pearl pin. His hair, normally so unkempt and wild, had been slicked back, and he had even taken off the crucifix which he normally wore in his right ear.

His whole apparel was wildly unconventional, and yet somehow right for him, and, even Angie had to admit, amazingly stylish. Angie couldn't imagine anyone else having the nerve to wear what JJ was wearing, or getting away with it so successfully.

There was only one word she could think of to describe the way JJ looked: a *star*.

"Wow," was all she could think of to say.

"Your carriage awaits you, my lady," he said in a put-on posh accent. He was holding an unfurled umbrella in his hand, to protect Angie from the heavy snow that was falling down all around them.

Angie forced herself to look past JJ and at the

waiting limousine. "JJ, how can you afford all this?" she asked. "You've only just released your first single! You're hardly the big time yet."

"That's right: Zone aren't big time yet," JJ admitted. "But Joe is."

"Joe Krupp laid all this on?" Angie asked in amazement as she allowed herself to be led to the waiting limo. Knowing how fiercely protective he was of his "boys", she couldn't imagine Zone's dictatorial manager sanctioning this sort of extravagance.

"Well, kind of," JJ said sheepishly and opened the passenger door for Angie.

"What do you mean 'kind of'?" Angie demanded.

"I booked the car over the phone on his own personal credit card account," JJ admitted. "I … er, just forgot to tell him about it before I did it…"

"He'll kill you when he finds out," Angie said, struggling not to laugh, or admire the young rock star's audacity.

"It's all worth it to impress a lovely lady!" he announced dramatically, and beneath his over-the-top manner Angie had the strangest idea that JJ actually meant what he was saying.

"So, where are we headed for?" she asked, once they were installed in the back seat of the limo, JJ had handed her a diet Coke from the in-car bar, and the chauffeur moved the limo silently off down the street.

"I told you," JJ said. "To the classiest joint I know of. It's about thirty miles out of town. And it's got the best cooking in the world!"

Angie could hardly wait. If the limo, and the chauffeur, and JJ's stunningly stylish and sexy suit – funny that, even in a suit she could still make out every line, every muscled contour, of his athletic body – if they were all a sample of what was to come, then tonight was going to be one classy night out to remember!

"Fried eggs and chips twice, please, Frank," JJ called out cheerfully.

The man behind the counter, a pot-bellied, unshaven man, a cigarette dangling from his lips, nodded. "You got it, JJ," he said, and repeated his order to the mousy woman by the chip-pan. He looked JJ up and down, clearly unimpressed by the young man's bizarre outfit.

"Say, who's died, JJ?" he asked jokingly. "You going to a funeral or what?"

"No one's died yet, Frank," JJ said cheerfully, and then turned around to look at Angie. *Although from the look on Angie's face I think the first one to die might just be me!* he thought.

Angie had been expecting to be taken to the grill room of the Birmingham Hilton, or the restaurant of some fancy country house. Nothing had prepared her for the greasy spoon caff JJ had taken her to.

She looked around in horror at the tiny formica tables, the rusty tea urn, and the piles of ready-buttered bread slices behind the serving counter.

On the wall hung a dog-eared calendar, with a photograph of a local boxing hero, and a hand-written notice advertising the caff's house

114

speciality breakfast of two eggs, sausage, bacon, mushroom, tomato and fried bread, at an extra-special cheap price if you ordered it before eight o'clock in the morning.

In fact, in Angie's eyes the greasy spoon had only two saving graces: it seemed reasonably clean, and apart from JJ and herself, and the two people she assumed were the owner and his wife, it was mercifully empty. At least no one would know she'd been here!

"Is this some sort of joke, JJ?" she demanded frostily.

JJ tried not to snigger at Angie's surprise and shook his head. "No. Here you get the best egg and chips anywhere in the world!"

"And this is your favourite restaurant?" Angie asked in disbelief.

JJ nodded happily, sadistically enjoying Angie's discomfort. "That's right," he said, and led her to one of the formica tables. He pulled out a wooden chair for her to sit down on. "Frank's Caff is my favourite place in the whole world."

Angie looked at JJ as if he was mad. "I demand to be taken home," she said. JJ shook his head.

"No can do," he said. "We're miles away from anywhere here, it's snowing outside, and I've sent the chauffeur away. He won't be back until ten-thirty!"

Angie was trapped and she knew it. Resigned to her fate, she sat down. It could be worse, she realized. At least her friends weren't here to see her in such a dump.

And then to her horror, the proprietor, Frank,

plonked an empty wine bottle on to their table, and lit the stump of a candle which he had stuck into its neck. He nodded over to his wife behind the counter, and as he lit the candle with his pocket lighter, she turned down the lights to create a more romantic atmosphere.

A few moments later, tinny, schmaltzy music came from the ghetto blaster from behind the counter, and Frank and his wife emerged from their tiny kitchen, carrying two plates piled high with egg and chips, and swimming in grease.

Angie felt her stomach heave at the thought of all that cholesterol, even though the food did smell good. *Almost good enough to eat*, she thought ironically.

Frank placed the two plates in front of Angie and her dinner date. "Enjoy!" he said.

Angie raised her eyes heavenwards and sighed. Some romantic evening this was turning out to be.

While Angie and JJ were eating their egg and chips, Rebecca Penswick was having the time of her life. When she'd returned home to her Aunt Lizzie's house there had been a message waiting for her on the ansaphone. It had been Adrian, inviting her out for the night.

Deciding that perhaps she had been a little mean to her boyfriend standing him up earlier in the afternoon, she agreed to meet up with him at Vito's, the bistro they had all been to on Christmas Eve.

When she arrived there she had been delighted

to find that he'd brought with him his cousin, Luke, as well as Danny and Marco, from Zone. The only girl among four such good-looking boys, she was flirting outrageously with each of them in turn, much to Adrian's evident distress.

As they drank more and more beer the boys began to tell her tales of the band, and especially of Krupp's big plans for them. Image was all-important for them, Krupp always said, and he had chosen an image for each of them, to go with their personalities, and which would help to market the band to as many people as possible.

Luke was meant to be the mean 'n' moody one, which was why he always wore designer stubble, ripped jeans, and a grubby T-shirt. Marco was the sensitive one, with his nose always buried deep in a book, even though anyone who had seen him with his shirt off on stage would have guessed correctly that he spent more of his free time in the gym than the local library. Young Danny with his cheeky smile and that baseball cap which he always wore back-to-front was supposed to be the cute one, the one that all the mothers would adore when they bought their daughters a Zone CD as a birthday present.

"And what about JJ?" asked Rebecca, wondering exactly what image Zone's manager had chosen for the sexiest member of the band.

"JJ's supposed to be the baaaad boy," Marco said, drawing out the adjective, "the one your mother always warned you about. He's unpredictable: you're never meant to know what he's going to do next. The sort of guy who kisses the girls and makes them cry…"

"When in fact he's just a big softie," Luke said, a little contemptuously. There had always been a rivalry between the two best-looking members of Zone, and Luke always welcomed the chance to stir things. "He'd never have asked your friend out, if we hadn't bet him that he couldn't do it!"

"*What?*" Rebecca was horrified by what she was hearing. "You bet JJ that he couldn't get Angie to go out with him?"

"Hey, it was just a joke," Danny said quickly, eager to clear up any misunderstanding. "We didn't mean anything by it."

"Oh, no?" Rebecca was unconvinced.

"JJ's not the sort of egomaniac you might think," Danny continued. "I've known him longer than the others. And he's a really nice unselfish guy."

"Music's his life," Marco agreed. "And if a girl says she won't go out with him then he takes it philosophically. After all, there are plenty of others who would be more than willing to date him."

"Then why is he chasing Angie?" Rebecca asked sternly. "If not for a bet?"

Danny shrugged. "Who knows? But I've never seen JJ go after any girl like this before … If I didn't know him better I'd say he was falling in love…"

"I'll kill you for this, you know, JJ," Angie said, and glared at her dining companion. She felt like a proper little idiot eating egg and chips in a greasy spoon while wearing a swanky silk dress that had cost her – or to be more precise her dad's credit card – hundreds of pounds.

"Wait until you've finished your meal," JJ said, and took a swig from the can of low-alcohol beer Frank had brought him. "Then you can kill me!"

In spite of herself, Angie laughed. And much as she hated to admit it, the eggs and chips tasted delicious. The chips especially were crisp and dry, not soggy and bland like the ones she'd occasionally had from the local chippy near college. She'd even asked Martha – Frank's wife – for a second helping, and Martha had been only too happy to oblige.

"You like?" JJ asked. He'd already finished his meal.

Angie nodded.

"I thought you would," JJ said. "Like I said, if you want good food Frank's Caff is the place to come."

"I'd never have thought of coming here in a hundred years," Angie admitted and mopped up the remains of her egg with the bread and butter Frank had thoughtfully provided her with. "And I would have imagined a pop star—"

"A third-rate pop star, I think you called me," JJ said.

"How did you know that?" Angie asked.

"Rebecca told Adrian," JJ said. "And Adrian told Luke. And Luke told me! That's three more people you can add to your list of people to kill!"

"Anyway I called you second-rate, not third-rate," Angie said smugly, "so don't put yourself down."

"I'll leave that to you then, shall I?" JJ countered, and grinned, enjoying this sparring with Angie.

"I'd never imagined someone like you in a place like this," Angie continued. "Maybe a trendy bistro or an upmarket hamburger joint, but not a greasy spoon miles away from anywhere."

"I've been coming here for years," JJ said. "Ever since I moved out here when my parents died…"

"I'm sorry…"

"You needn't be," JJ said. "But you see, Angie, you should never judge by appearances. I mean, who would have thought that someone as pretty as you could be such a successful student journalist?"

Angie groaned and put down her knife and fork. "Do you know that was the tackiest line I have ever heard in my entire life?" she asked in all seriousness.

JJ nodded happily. "It was worth it though," he said, and then added, much more seriously: "And what's more, I meant it."

Angie blushed. There was something about JJ which fascinated her. Away from the other boys he wasn't half as brash and macho as he pretended to be. And he made her laugh too. That was something that only a few other boys could do.

"I need a favour, JJ," she said.

"I thought there might be a catch," JJ joked. "I knew you wouldn't let me take you out to this glamorous five-star restaurant without asking for something in return!" He sighed, and placed his hand on his chest, as though he were heart-broken. "There I was thinking you'd agreed to come out with me because of my charm, my wit, and my undeniable sophistication. I should have known that there had to be an ulterior motive!"

"Pig," said Angie jokingly. "Listen, JJ, I've got a big problem."

"Too right you have," JJ agreed. "You're going out with a prize geek when you could be going out with me."

"Maybe," Angie said.

Maybe? What am I talking about? I've got every-thing I want in Dominic!

"JJ, I do some work at Cuttleigh Hall."

"That little place on the outskirts of town?" he asked.

"How do you know about that?" she asked, curious.

"I come from round here, remember?" he said. "Nurse Clare is famous in these parts. She looks after the disabled kids, doesn't she?"

"That's right. Well, I'm organizing a New Year's Eve party for the boys and girls there," she told him. "Streamers, balloons, party games, that sort of thing. I'd booked a conjurer to entertain them…"

"That's a great idea," said JJ, and sighed wist-fully. "I used to love it when Mum and Dad took me to see magicians at the fairground … before they died…"

"But he's cried off at the last moment," Angie

explained. "Nurse Clare rang me up to tell me that he's caught this flu bug that's going round."

JJ looked warily at Angie. "And?" he asked.

God, he's enjoying this! Angie thought. *He knows exactly what I'm going to ask him and he's really enjoying watching me squirm!*

She leaned forward to look JJ straight in the eyes. Those eyes the colour of autumn leaves. He was wearing a sweet-smelling cologne, and for a second she was reminded of the fragrance Dominic usually wore. Dominic's was a much more manly smell; JJ's was a more feminine, more unpredictable fragrance, but he wore it with style and it suited him well.

"JJ, I need someone to entertain those kids," she pleaded. "Their whole day will be ruined if we don't put on a show for them!"

"Now let me see if I've got this straight," JJ said slowly. "You want Zone – tipped to be the next big thing in pop music – you want Zone to be the entertainers at a scrappy little kids' party?"

Angie nodded. The way he put it, it did sound a pretty dumb idea.

"You want me to persuade the other guys to give up their New Year's Eve?" He whistled. "That's a pretty tall order, Angie."

"I know," Angie said, and hung her head. She'd been an idiot to even think of the idea.

"Joe will never let us do it, you know; not unless you're paying big money up front."

"Er, that's another problem. It's a charity gig," she admitted. "You might get leftover jelly and cake if you're lucky..."

122

"Which I can take back and eat in my playpen, I guess?" he said, reminding Angie of her Christmas Eve put-down in Vito's.

"Er, yes…"

JJ took Angie's hand in his; she didn't try to move it away. "Angie, tell me the truth," he said softly. "You wouldn't have agreed to come out with me tonight if it hadn't been to ask me to do this gig?"

Angie wanted to turn away. Instead, she looked straight into JJ's face. "You're right, JJ," she said guiltily. "I'm sorry…"

Or am I? Or am I using the party as an excuse?

JJ stared at her for a moment, as though he was trying to see into her mind, as though he was trying to understand just what Angie was about. She'd just gone and told him the truth, straight out, and not got flustered and come up with excuses or lies. He liked that, he liked that a lot.

Angie returned his stare, and gazed into JJ's eyes, expecting to find there anger, or, at the very least, disappointment. Instead, she saw a flash of delight – and something else too.

JJ took his hand away from Angie's.

"OK," he said simply.

"What?" Angie asked.

"I said OK. We'll do the gig, on New Year's Eve, in two days' time."

"You mean it?" she gasped. "You really mean it?"

"I just said so, didn't I?" JJ was smiling, and seemed almost as delighted as Angie was.

123

"JJ, this is terrific!" she said. "You are such a great guy!" She leaned over and kissed him.

Kissed him on the lips.

She pulled sharply away, realizing what she'd just done. Without even thinking. Realizing that it had just felt like the most natural thing to do in the world. Realizing that it was what she had wanted to do for days now, ever since she had interviewed JJ in that shabby little dressing room.

What was it Steph had once said to her? Something about how she thought Peter Markowska was the most insufferable man she had ever met. Pompous, arrogant, and self-opinionated. And that how, one day, she realized that it was all an act to hide the shy and frightened man underneath.

She'd said something about opposites attracting.

Something about magnets and iron.

Don't be stupid, Angie! she reprimanded herself. *He's nothing more than a randy rock star on the make! And you've got Dominic now! What abut him? How would sweet, kind, unselfish Dominic feel if he knew what you were doing now?*

Nevertheless, she kissed JJ again on the lips, briefly, only for a second, before JJ – and not Angie – pulled away. They looked at each other for a half-instant, neither of them quite knowing what to say, but each of them understanding everything.

Finally JJ stood up and looked at his watch. It was half-past ten and outside their limo was waiting.

"C'mon, Angie," he said, "I've got to drive you home." He sighed. "And then I've got some major work to do on Danny, Luke and Marco! It's going to be tough to persuade them to give up their partying."

"It's only for the afternoon," Angie pointed out. "They can still go out on New Year's Eve night."

"Aha, but these guys like to party all day," JJ said. "After all, you know what they all say about rock stars, don't you?"

He came round to her side of the table, and took her hand, leading her to the door like a courtier escorting a duchess to the races.

Unseen by Angie, Frank and his wife winked at JJ as he led her out of the door.

Outside in the cold and the snow, JJ and Angie hurried to the limo. As she climbed into the passenger seat Angie turned to JJ, who was holding the door open for her. "Thank you, JJ," she said. "You've been really sweet. You're a really nice guy."

"Just don't spread it around," JJ said in a stage whisper. "It'll ruin my image!"

They laughed, and then JJ suddenly became serious. "And congratulations, Angie," he said mysteriously. "You've just passed the test."

Angie frowned, unsure what JJ was saying. Even when he had dropped her off at her house, and given her a friendly goodnight peck on the cheek, she still wasn't sure what he had meant.

Passed the test? Passed what test? What did JJ mean?

10

"Well, how do I look?" Angie asked Rebecca, as she waltzed into Aunt Lizzie's sitting room, and did a twirl. She was wearing a tan Dolce è Gabanna dress, and matching brown leather boots.

Rebecca looked up from her copy of John Donne's love poems, and nodded approvingly.

"You look wonderful, Angie," she said, truthfully, and a little jealously too. Angie, after all, would look good in a sack. "Who's the lucky boy tonight?"

"Dominic," Angie said. "What do you mean, who's the lucky boy tonight? Of course, it's Dominic. Who else could it be?"

Rebecca closed her book and looked up mischievously at Angie. "I just thought that after your date with JJ last night..."

"Listen, Rebecca Penswick," laughed Angie, sitting down on the sofa next to her friend. In the background music was softly playing: Rebecca was listening to the local pop music station. "That was just a friendly evening out! There's nothing to be read into it!"

"Oh, no?" asked Rebecca. "That's not what I've heard…"

"What do you mean?" Angie asked urgently. How could Rebecca have heard about that "thank-you" kiss that she had given JJ? How could she have known about the way her heart had beaten so much that she thought it would burst whenever she was close to JJ in that greasy spoon? Had JJ – that louse – been bragging?

"Marco told me," Rebecca replied. "He rang me this morning to tell me that JJ hadn't stopped talking about you since last night. Told me how they're all going to give a concert at Cuttleigh Hall tomorrow afternoon."

Angie clapped her hands with delight. "That's great news!" she whooped. "I knew JJ could talk them round to the idea!" she said admiringly.

"He said that JJ had been trying to get in touch with you all day to tell you," Rebecca added.

"I was putting in some work on the *Recorder*, and then I was out buying this dress," Angie said, and then frowned. "Wait a minute. What's Marco doing ringing you up?" The penny dropped, and she gave her friend one of her most disapproving looks. "Oh, Bec, you haven't gone and dumped Adrian for Marco, have you?"

"Of course not," Rebecca said, a little guiltily, and not very convincingly. "But Marco and I get on so well together. He's such a nice guy – all the boys in Zone are – and we had a really good time together in Vito's last night." She glanced down at the book of love poetry. "And we like so many of the same things – poetry, music…"

Angie nodded sagely, realizing that within the next few days Adrian was going to get what she termed as the Big Heave-Ho. He and Rebecca had been going out for practically three weeks now: it was almost a record on Rebecca's part!

And she also knew that Rebecca was not a mean-spirited person and that, when she did break it off with Adrian, it would be in the nicest and gentlest way possible. Rebecca had had many boyfriends, and every single one of them still remained on good and friendly terms with her.

Rebecca pointed to the thin cardboard folder Angie was holding. "Some romantic evening with Dominic it's going to be, if you're going to be talking schoolwork all the time!" she said.

"We won't be," Angie said, and took two sheets of computer print-out paper out of the folder. She showed them to Rebecca: they contained a list of names and addresses.

"I promised Dominic I'd get him a list of fashion contacts," Angie said. "You know – so he can try and make it as a model."

"I thought your dad wouldn't help him out," Rebecca said, puzzled.

"Well, he didn't," Angie said shamefacedly. "He and Steph were out last night..."

"So you took them from his Filofax when you got back from your date with JJ!"

Angie shook her head smugly. "No. Dad doesn't go anywhere without his Filofax."

"So how?"

"Dad's so absent-minded at times that Steph is

convinced that he's going to lose his Filo one day," Angie explained. "So she's transferred all his contact numbers on to her computer. These sheets of paper are a print-out of his contacts in the fashion business!"

"You crafty ace reporter!" Rebecca said admiringly, before adding: "They'll kill you if they find out, you know."

"Well, they won't, unless you tell them, will they?" Angie said.

"My lips are sealed," Rebecca said. "You know I always keep secrets."

"That's right," Angie agreed. "You're a good friend, Rebecca. One of the very best."

Rebecca's face fell, as she remembered what Marco had told her over the telephone that morning. When JJ had rejoined the others in their hotel last night, he had found out how the guys had let slip that they had challenged him to take Angie out on a date. JJ had exploded and warned that Angie was never to find out about that.

When Marco had phoned Rebecca up he had sworn her to secrecy also. Rebecca was now torn between loyalty to her best friend and her promise to keep a secret.

"So, where did you say Dominic Dreamboat was taking you tonight?" she asked, in order to take her mind off her dilemma.

"Oh, just Vincente's," Angie said, casually, as though she was talking about a tiny corner restaurant.

"That's right!" Rebecca marvelled. "The poshest

restaurant in town! He must be really serious about you, Angie!"

"Yes," said Angie, "I think he is..."

On the radio, the DJ stopped prattling to his listeners and flipped on another CD. A familiar, dreamy tune emerged from the speakers, the tune Angie and Dominic had danced to together at the Christmas dance. It seemed suddenly that JJ was singing just for Angie:

> Ask me once, and I'd give you the moon,
>   For you're my best girl, and you know it's true;
> The other guys might fool you, make you dance
>   to their tune
>   But, my love, I'd be lost without you.

"You look wonderful, Angie," Dominic said, and held her hands across the table at Vincente's.

All around them, impeccably dressed waiters minced about, carrying aloft huge silver trays, displaying some of the most delicious-looking dishes that could be had for miles around. A wine-waiter was always on hand to ensure that their glasses were never empty, and in the corner a string quartet played an unobtrusive selection of classical tunes. It was as far removed as it was possible to be from the caff JJ had taken her to.

"Thank you, Dominic," Angie said, her cheeks flushed a little from the wine she had been drinking. "It's been a wonderful meal."

"It wouldn't have been half so wonderful without your company," he said, and gazed into her eyes.

Dominic's own eyes were a startling, brilliant blue, real model's eyes: it was funny, but Angie always forgot just how blue they were until she saw him again. They were much more brilliant than JJ's hazel eyes, the colour of autumn leaves after the rain.

"I don't want this to end," Angie said, as their waiter brought them two espressos to round off their meal. "But we both need early nights: we've both got a busy day tomorrow..."

"Sorry?"

"I've got the children's party at Cuttleigh to organize, remember?" she said. "And you've got to make an early start to go and visit your grandmother."

"Oh, yes..." he said.

Angie stroked his hand sympathetically. "I know it's selfish of me, but I can't pretend that I'm not disappointed about you not being able to help me with the party," she said. "But I understand. I really am very sorry about your grandmother. Is she very ill?"

"Gran?" Dominic asked absently, as though his mind was somewhere else. "Her doctors say she's only got a few more weeks to live," he said. "This will probably be the last time I see her alive..."

Angie lifted Dominic's hands to her mouth and kissed them. "I've brought something with me which might cheer you up," she said.

She reached down under the table and picked up the cardboard folder: Dominic had noticed it when she first arrived at the restaurant but hadn't remarked upon it. She handed it over to him.

"Don't tell anyone I've given you this," she warned. "Otherwise I'm going to get into the most enormous trouble!"

"What is it?" he asked excitedly, as he took out the two sheets of computer print-out, and cast his eyes down the list of names.

"My dad's contact list of anyone who's anyone in the fashion business," she said. "Home phone numbers, fax numbers, the works! If these people can't get you a modelling contract then no one can!"

"Angie, this is absolutely fantastic!" Dominic gasped. "How can I ever thank you?"

"I'll think of something," she said.

Dominic leaned over the table to kiss her, a warm, brief kiss on the lips. Angie reached out her hand, and pulled him back to her, for a longer, more passionate kiss. Dominic pulled away, and grinned.

"Whoa, not here, Angie," he said, and glanced shyly at the other posh-looking diners in the restaurant. "What would people think?"

Dominic chuckled and replaced the two sheets of paper in the cardboard folder. He signalled to the waiter for the bill.

"Are we going now?" Angie asked, and looked down at her unfinished espresso. "I wish this night could go on for ever."

"I'm afraid so," said Dominic. "Like you said, we've both got early starts tomorrow." He rolled up the cardboard folder and put it in the inside pocket of his jacket, and smiled gratefully at Angie. "And thank you, Angie, thank you from the bottom of my heart!"

11

Zone are terrific, Angie decided, the funkiest, most exciting and good-looking group she had ever seen, and the kids at Cuttleigh were having the time of their lives as the band performed for them on the makeshift stage at the New Year's Eve party.

And JJ is one of the most charismatic performers I've ever seen! she added to herself.

JJ, whether he was singing steamy rockers or sultry ballads, had his audience in the palm of his hand. He flirted with the young teenage girls, was silly and childish with the younger ones, and winked conspiratorially at the boys when he sang some of his more rebellious lyrics.

Cuttleigh was a small institution and there were only about sixty children in the audience; but JJ and Zone played as if they were performing in front of a crowd of tens of thousands at Wembley Arena, or the Hollywood Bowl.

Zone's act included a section where JJ selected one member of the audience to dance with on stage. As he sang her a love song, promising her that she was the only girl in the world, and gazing dreamily into her eyes, she instantly became the most envied member of the audience. All the girls wished that they could be there, up on stage, with that impossibly sexy man, singing of his wish that this dance could go on for ever.

At Cuttleigh JJ picked on a young girl in a wheelchair. Getting her wheelchair on stage would have posed a problem, so JJ simply leapt off the stage, lifted her up out of the wheelchair, and danced with her in his arms.

Angie brushed a tear from her eye, and hoped that no one had noticed. That JJ had picked someone in a wheelchair to dance with, rather than a more able-bodied person, was wonderful; that he had somehow intuitively zeroed in on the shyest and most insecure girl in the entire building, and was now making her smile like Angie had never seen her smile before, was little short of miraculous.

"The lucky thing," Rebecca said. "What I wouldn't give to be dancing with JJ!"

"He's marvellous," Angie agreed. "And he's so at ease with the kids."

Angie had seen other people give performances at Cuttleigh, and she had often remarked that they were uncomfortable around some of the more seriously disabled children. But JJ showed no such distress, and didn't even seem to notice their disabilities. So much for the image of the dangerous, irresponsible and unpredictable rock star which Joe Krupp was trying so hard to promote!

When Zone finished their hour-long set – Angie and JJ had agreed on twenty-five minutes, but, as he had warned her, once Zone started enjoying themselves they could go on for ever – they didn't leave for their dressing room (which was, in fact, Nurse Clare's office). Instead they jumped off stage and started mingling with their audience, signing autographs, chatting and joking, acting not like stars, but just like the boys you might bump into down at the local youth club.

Rebecca patted Angie on the back. "Well done," she said. "It's been the most successful party ever. Although Heaven knows how the boys got Joe Krupp to agree to them playing here – and for free!"

"I don't care how," Angie said, and pointed out JJ.

JJ was holding a young three-year-old toddler in his arms. He looked totally incongruous, dressed in his leathers, his sweat-drenched shirt open to the waist, as he gave the delighted little girl a kiss on the cheek. Suddenly he was aware of Angie looking at him, and he winked at her, and smiled with flawlessly white teeth.

"He's incredible," Angie gushed. "The way he treats the kids. Who'd've thought it?"

"Who indeed?" said Rebecca, looking suspiciously at her friend. Over by the stage, Adrian had been helping with the sound system, and he came over to join them.

"Thanks, Adrian," Angie said. "You were a great help, coming in at such short notice." Adrian nodded as if to say: *No problem*.

"Wasn't Marco great on keyboards?" Rebecca asked, and Adrian sighed.

Angie smiled. It seemed like Rebecca and Adrian had already had a quiet word about the future of their relationship; and, as she had guessed, they were still remaining good friends.

"I was expecting to see Dominic Cairns here," Adrian said. "Couldn't he make it?"

"His grandmother is seriously ill," Angie explained. "He's gone to see her for the New Year."

Rebecca and Adrian exchanged puzzled looks. "Are you sure, Angie?" Rebecca asked.

Before Angie had the chance to reply, Nurse Clare came up to them. She kissed Angie gratefully on both cheeks, and gave her a hug.

"My poppet, you were superb!" the Scottish woman enthused. "The children loved the musicians!"

"They're called Zone, Nurse Clare," Angie smiled. "And they're going to be very famous very soon."

"I couldn't bear the noise myself," Nurse Clare said frankly; "give me the bagpipes any day." And then she sighed philosophically. "But it's what you young ones want today, I suppose. And I must thank you for bringing the lost sheep back into the fold, if only for the day."

"Huh?" Angie didn't have the slightest idea what Nurse Clare was talking about.

Nurse Clare nodded over to JJ, who was still surrounded by a crowd of adoring and giggling children.

"It was so nice to see Jeremy again. The children do love him so: he was always very good with them, you know."

"*Jeremy?*"

"That's right." Nurse Clare couldn't understand the look of amazement on the faces of Angie, Rebecca and Adrian. "Don't you recall me telling you about him? One of our best voluntary workers until he left town a few years ago."

Angie looked back at the hunky, leather-clad figure of JJ, trying to reconcile the music scene's latest bad boy with that of the unselfish and diligent voluntary care worker, whom Nurse Clare praised so effusively. So that explained JJ's ease among the children, and the wonderful way he communicated with them.

JJ was Jeremy?

She saw JJ catch their eyes, and he made his way through the crowd towards them, still carrying the little girl in his arms. He was beaming from ear to ear. Angie didn't think she'd ever seen him looking so happy as he did now.

"Hi, girls; hi, Adrian," he said, and then kissed the septuagenarian director of Cuttleigh on the cheek. "And it's really nice to see you again, Nurse Clare."

Angie glared at the young rock star. "JJ," she said frostily. "We have to talk – *now!*"

"Hey, c'mon, babe, what's the big deal?" JJ said as Angie furiously led him to Nurse Clare's office.

"The big deal," said Angie as she slammed the door shut, "is that you lied to me! And don't call me babe!"

"What do you mean, 'lied' to you?" JJ was confused and felt not in control; and that made him just as angry as Angie.

"You didn't tell me that you used to work here!" she said. "You didn't tell me the sort of person you really are!"

JJ looked at Angie as if he thought she was mad. And then it clicked. "Aha, I see what's eating you up so much, Miss Ace Reporter!" he shouted. "You don't like the wool being pulled over your eyes, do you? You don't like being made a fool of, do you!"

"Of course not," Angie protested. "I mean, of course..." She shuddered with rage. "I don't know what I feel!"

"You thought I was the 'bad boy', didn't you?" JJ continued cruelly. "You believed all the PR rubbish Joe's put out, didn't you? That's your trouble, Angie, you've judged me by what you *think* I am, and not who I am! You thought I was just another big-headed pop star—"

"No," she lied.

"Another big-headed pop star who thought he'd try out his luck on the budding female reporter, see if he could add another notch to his bedpost!"

Angie was dumbstruck. She was so used to boys flattering her, complimenting her, hoping maybe for a date; no boy had ever spoken to her like this before.

"Well, let me tell you, *babe*," JJ continued, and pointed an angry accusing finger at Angie. "I could have any girl I wanted. And no, I'm not being big-headed now, it's the truth!"

Angie nodded meekly: she knew JJ was right.

"But I chose you, *babe*, I decided to go after you, *babe*, someone who was so high and mighty that she wouldn't even look at me twice—"

No, it wasn't like that, Angie thought tearfully. *I thought you were so big-headed that I wouldn't give you the chance to show me who you really were. I didn't want you or the others in Zone to see that I was like everybody else, I didn't want to make a fool of myself. But I was attracted to you from the very first moment I saw you.*

"I chose to make a compete idiot of myself in front of my best mates, in front of your friends," JJ raged, "and all because ... all because..."

"Yes, JJ?" Angie asked softly, hopefully.

JJ shrugged self-consciously, and turned his hazel-coloured eyes away from Angie.

"All because I think I might be falling in love with you..."

An enormous silence fell on the room. JJ raised his head and looked at Angie. There were tears in her eyes; or at least he thought there were, for there were tears in his as well, and everything seemed misty. Angie took a step towards him, and reached out a trembling hand to touch him on the shoulder.

"JJ, I don't know what to say..."

"There's nothing to say," he said sullenly, and turned away. Angie pulled him back, and forced him to look at her.

"You're right," she said. "I thought you were conceited and arrogant and a thousand other things too. And I couldn't understand why I was so attracted to you…"

"You were?" JJ, the future bad boy of British pop, the guy whose picture, everyone predicted, would be pinned up on everyone's bedroom walls within nine months, couldn't believe his ears.

"And that's why I ran from you," Angie admitted. "I thought you were all wrong for me, and I didn't want to make an idiot of myself. That's why I ignored the flowers, and the tapes, and Rebecca begging me to go out with you—"

"But you did in the end."

"Because I wanted something from you," Angie said, and then corrected herself. "No, not from you. From *what* you are."

"From me as a member of Zone, you mean."

Angie nodded. "But if I hadn't I'd've never seen the sort of person you are," she said. "I'd never have seen just how sweet, and kind, and loving you really are…"

JJ chuckled. "Don't tell anyone, will you?"

Angie smiled too. "Come here, JJ," she said.

Angie wrapped her arms around JJ, drawing his face to hers. Their lips sought each other out hungrily, and they kissed, a long, deep and tender kiss that took both their breaths away.

Angie looked up into JJ's face: into his hazel-brown eyes, ringed with long lashes, at his shock of dark-blond hair, wet and shiny with sweat, at his beardless firm jaw, and that divine little dimple in the centre of his chin.

"It's only ever been you," she whispered. "Since the beginning." She giggled. "Since you found me in your dressing room."

"When I found you there, I couldn't believe that anyone could have gone to those lengths to get an interview with me. You were different from all the others. You were intelligent, had a mind of your own – you knew what you wanted and you went out there and got it."

"No, JJ," Angie said. "I didn't know what I wanted – until now."

They kissed again, and Angie ran her hand down the small of JJ's back, over his shoulder-blades, then up along his smooth arms and his powerful biceps. She felt his body against hers, felt him breathing out as she breathed in. He nuzzled her neck, nibbling the lobe of her ear, blowing gently into her ear.

Shudders of delight coursed through Angie's entire body. She could have been on another planet. If Rebecca, Adrian, Nurse Clare, if even her dad and Stephanie and Joe Krupp had walked in now, she wouldn't have moved, wouldn't have strayed from the side of this gorgeous man, this blond-haired, pale-faced man who was the exact opposite of her "type", and who she knew now she loved, loved against all reason, loved against all sense, loved against every rule in the book of love.

She broke away from his embrace, and twined her fingers in his dark-blond hair, twisting it into little ringlets.

"Jeremy," she whispered and laughed.

JJ nodded. "Uh-huh," he said. "That's my name. Jeremy Jones."

"But why change it in the first place? And why keep it so secret?"

"Is this an interview, Ms Markowska?" he asked, only half-jokingly. "Hardly anyone knows my real name. Danny's one of the few who do, but then we've known each other for years now."

"This isn't an interview, JJ," Angie promised. "This is very definitely off the record."

JJ smiled, and Angie felt him relax slightly in her arms.

"Jeremy Jones is hardly a suitable name for a sleazy rocker, is it?" he asked. "It was Joe Krupp's idea."

Joe Krupp again. He seemed to control every aspect of the boys' lives.

"How did you persuade Joe to let you do this gig in the first place?" she asked him curiously.

"I have my ways," JJ said mysteriously.

"Tell me!" Angie demanded.

"The ace reporter will have to find that out for herself, won't she?" JJ teased. "But I did this gig for two reasons. For the kids, because I used to work here..."

"Nurse Clare told me you stopped working here several years ago," Angie remembered. "Why did you leave if you loved it so much?"

"My parents died in a car crash, five years ago when I was fifteen," he said. "My aunt and uncle became my guardians after that. When they moved away from the area, I couldn't afford to live here on my own. So I went with them. And I stayed with them, helping them run their business, until last year when Joe Krupp spotted

143

me singing in a local talent contest and asked me to join Zone."

"So you helped them in their business," Angie said, and remembered the conversation they had shared in the greasy spoon two nights ago. Then he had told Angie that singing was his only life, that he couldn't do anything else.

JJ laughed again, and gave his girlfriend – for with a shock he realized that that was exactly what Angie had become in the past few glorious minutes – a brief peck on the lips.

"Their business isn't the sort of business you have in mind, Angie," he said. "They don't work in TV like your dad, or at the local college like your stepmother."

"So what do they do?" Angie asked. "How did you help them in their business?"

"I served the egg and chips."

"What?" asked Angie, and JJ laughed at her surprise. "Wait a minute, you don't mean that greasy spoon – I mean, that café we went to the other night—"

"Which you turned your nose up at when you first crossed over the threshold, because it wasn't what you were expecting, but where you were polite and charming and considerate to Frank and Martha who run the place, because you didn't want to hurt their feelings... And what's more you asked Martha for a second helping."

"They're your uncle and aunt?" Angie asked, amazed. "They looked after you when your mum and dad died?"

JJ nodded. "That's right, Angie. You see, you

shouldn't judge by appearances. Remember what I told you at the end of that evening?"

Angie nodded; his words had been puzzling her ever since. "You told me that I'd passed the test…"

"I've taken other girls there," JJ said, "and every one of them has turned her nose up at the place, and demanded to be taken to Vito's or Vincente's, or some other posh joint. And sure, I took them where they wanted to go; but I never saw them again."

"It wouldn't have mattered where I was," Angie said, "as long as I was with you."

"We fought for half of the meal!" JJ reminded her.

"I know. And I enjoyed every minute of it!" she said.

"Frank and Martha loved you, Angie," JJ said. "You passed the test all right. You passed the test with flying colours!"

Suddenly they both started as the door opened. They sprang from each other's embrace, but not before Rebecca, standing in the doorway, had the chance to take in the situation.

"There you are, JJ," she said. "I've been looking all over for you. Nurse Clare says if you wouldn't mind signing a few more autographs…"

"Sure, why not?" JJ said, and headed for the door. "I'll see you girls later, OK?" He waved them goodbye and winked at Angie.

As soon as he had gone Rebecca turned to her best friend. "So?" was all she needed to say.

"So what?" asked Angie and grinned. Nothing

else needed to be said between the two of them.

"Well, well, well, what a dark horse you are, Angie," Rebecca said admiringly. "You tell me off for fancying Adrian and Marco. But at least I drop Adrian before I start going out with Marco. Even I don't keep two boyfriends on the go at the same time!"

Dominic Cairns! In the euphoria of the past fifteen minutes Angie had forgotten that Dominic even existed. Dominic was so different from JJ that it sometimes seemed that they lived in two separate worlds.

Angie was going to be forced to choose between the two of them. But how could she make the choice about two people who were as different from each other as could be? How could she make her decision?

12

Angie slammed the phone down for the third time that morning. It seemed that neither Dominic nor his parents were at home, and all she could get was their ansaphone. She frowned as she remembered that Dominic had told her that they wouldn't be staying the night at his grandmother's and that they would be back very late on New Year's Eve.

Now it was New Year's Day, and still there had been no reply from Dominic. She had wanted to wish him a Happy New Year, hoping that this year would be the best for both of them, and when she received no answer she started to worry that Dominic's grandmother might have taken a turn for the worse; she was sure that if she had he would have altered his plans to stay with the old lady. But why hadn't he told her? Why didn't he realize how concerned she was about him?

Angie picked up the phone again and prepared to dial the number of JJ's hotel. She had had a restless night, even turning down the New Year's

Eve party Rebecca had invited her to. How could she enjoy herself when at the back of her mind was the nagging question: *Dominic? Or JJ?* She had to chose between the two of them: she knew that it wasn't fair on either of them or on herself.

JJ knew that she had been out with Dominic, certainly, but he didn't realize just how much she felt for the captain of the football team. And yet every time she went out with Dominic, she found herself comparing him with JJ, seeing JJ's hazel-coloured eyes when she looked into Dominic's (funny how she still couldn't remember what colour his eyes were), smelling JJ's fragrance whenever Dominic was near to her, thinking how messy and unkempt JJ's hair was when compared to Dominic's.

She started to dial when the door to her bedroom opened. Her father was standing there, an angry look on his face.

"You. Downstairs. Now," he said abruptly, and stormed off to the study where Stephanie was waiting for them. With a sinking heart Angie followed him.

"I thought I told you that the information in my Filofax was totally confidential," he told her. He had his Filofax in his hand and was waving it angrily in his daughter's face.

"You did," Angie said. "And it is." What was the big deal?

"Then why have you been taking names and addresses from my list of contacts?" Mr Markowska demanded.

"I haven't been anywhere near your blasted

Filofax, Dad," Angie protested.

"You've accessed the information contained in it and which was stored on Stephanie's computer though, haven't you?" he accused her. Angie looked over at Stephanie, who was standing by her computer.

Angie wished the ground could swallow her up. "How could you know...?"

Stephanie shook her head sadly. "I'm disappointed in you, Angie," she said and pointed to a small text box in the top left hand corner of the screen. "I found this when I switched on my monitor this morning," she explained. "It's a record of the last document which was worked on, and the time it was accessed."

Angie looked at the message in the box: FASHION/ TEL: 30 DECEMBER: 17.19. Sure enough the computer had recorded the time she had opened her Dad's file, and taken the information for Dominic. Angie kicked herself. How could she have been so stupid?

"Would you like to explain what you were doing rooting around in my personal files, young lady?" her father demanded, trying hard to control his temper.

Angie decided that honesty was the best policy. "Dominic is going to have a great career one day," she said. "All he needs is a little help ... All I gave him were a few addresses."

"Which you gave him against my express wishes?" asked her father.

Angie hung her head in shame. "Well, yes..." she admitted. "But Dominic's a good person, Dad, he'll be very discreet when he rings those people up. And it would be so nice to see him being successful in the fashion world..."

Peter Markowska harrumphed, but in truth he loved his daughter so much that he found it difficult to be annoyed with Angie for long.

"I'm sure Dominic will be discreet," he said. "I told you before, his father's a friend of mine. A more respected, upstanding family I couldn't hope to know..."

Stephanie placed a hand on her husband's shoulder. "Peter, why don't you let me handle this," she said softly. "Sort of – woman to woman?"

Peter nodded and left the room. As soon as he had closed the door Stephanie looked sternly at her stepdaughter.

"Don't think that just because I'm not shouting at you like your father I'm any the less angry with you, Angie," she said.

"I'm sorry, Steph..."

"Why did you do it, Angie?"

"I told you. I wanted to help Dominic. It wasn't as though he asked me: it was my own idea."

"And are you and he serious about each other?" Stephanie asked.

Angie paused. Yesterday morning she would have answered "yes" without even thinking. After the events of the previous day – after JJ – she wasn't so certain.

"Yes, we are," she said finally. "He's such a kind person. Modest, down-to-earth, neat and tidy. Not like some people I know..."

Not like JJ, she thought. *Nothing like JJ in a million years.*

"Good, I'm pleased for you," said Stephanie. "Your father and I would like to meet him sometime. Maybe you should invite him round."

"Yeah, sure," Angie said. She knew that Stephanie and her father would like Dominic. He was solid and reliable, just like Guy, her previous boyfriend, whom they had both adored.

She smiled: she dreaded to think what their reaction would be if she brought JJ round for tea in his leathers and his untidy mop of hair. Her father, who was always so protective of her, would probably have a coronary!

"Why not ring him now?" Stephanie asked. "Invite him around this evening?"

"I tried ringing him before," she said. "He's still not back from his grandmother's."

"That's nice," Stephanie approved. "Spending your New Year's Eve with your grandmother."

"Yeah, it is," Angie agreed. "And he is nice."

"Let's not say anything more about the matter of those phone numbers," said Stephanie. "All girls make idiots of themselves over a boy at one time or another. I know I certainly have."

"You?" Angie couldn't quite believe it: Stephanie was usually so sensible and level-headed.

"When I was your age, Angie – a long, long time ago – there was this boy at university I was crazy about. We went out together, and I thought he really loved me." Stephanie sighed, "I did everything for him, even helped him out with his essays and research. Until I found out he was going out with someone behind my back..."

"That's sad," said Angie.

"Not really," Stephanie said. "He was only going out with me so I could help him with his grades and exams. I was much cleverer than him, you see ... When I found out I felt like the biggest fool on the planet. But I got over it, and I learnt my lesson ... So let's forget about the phone numbers and start this New Year the way we mean to go on. OK?"

"Thanks, Steph," Angie said, and gratefully kissed her stepmother. She turned to go but Stephanie asked her to wait.

"There was a phone call for you early this morning," she said, and searched around her desk for the yellow sticker on which she had made a note of the caller's name. "Some boy ... He was lucky I was up so early working on some papers."

Some boy? Dominic? JJ?

"He said he wanted to be the first to wish you a Happy New Year, but I told him you were still in bed," Stephanie said, and finally found the note hidden underneath a pile of research papers.

"He sounded quite shy on the phone: I got the feeling that he wasn't quite sure whether you wanted to speak to him or not. He seemed relieved when I told you you'd gone to bed early and hadn't gone out partying..."

"Well, don't keep me in suspense all day, Steph!" Angie laughed. "Who was it? Who wanted to be the first person to wish me a Happy New Year? Was it Dominic? JJ?"

"JJ?" Stephanie looked down at the piece of paper on which she had scribbled the caller's name. "No, Angie, it wasn't JJ."

"Then who was it?"

"Jeremy," said Stephanie. "He said his name was Jeremy."

She looked up at Angie, caught the look of delighted surprise on her stepdaughter's face. "Angie, who is Jeremy?"

"Someone who trusts me, Steph," Angie said, and felt her eyes mist over with tears. "Someone who trusts me more than anyone else in the entire world."

13

"I didn't think you'd come," said JJ, who had been waiting at the bus stop for half an hour now. The shoulders of his leather jacket were covered with snow, and a wisp of hair hung out from the baseball cap which he had borrowed from Danny and which he was wearing to protect his head from the snowfall.

"It's New Year's Day," Angie said, as she stepped off the bus and it drove speedily away. "Everything's delayed by the holiday traffic and the snow." She kissed him on the lips. She shivered. "You're cold."

"You'll have to warm me up then," he said. The words were ones the old JJ might have used; the tone of voice in which he said it was something only the new JJ was capable of.

They held each other close, and kissed again. JJ tasted warm, and sweet, and loving, and the feel of his muscular arms wrapping tightly around her made Angie feel safe and secure, and as warm in the falling snow as she might have been on some tropical beach.

"Happy New Year," she breathed, and added mischievously: "Jeremy."

JJ screwed up his eyes in an effort to look menacing. "I trusted you with the biggest secret in the world," he snarled. "And if you call me Jeremy one more time I'll kill you!"

Angie was clearly unimpressed. "Sorry – *babe*," she said.

They burst into a fit of giggles and walked, arm-in-arm down the winding country lane.

Angie looked around. JJ had suggested they meet some distance away from town, in a small village well off the beaten track.

He knew a great village pub there where they could have a late lunch, he had said, when she had returned his call and rung his hotel room; and where there was little chance of him being recognized. Curiously enough, it was very close to the place where Angie had also met Dominic; she wondered how his grandmother was feeling now.

"I love coming out here," JJ said, almost echoing Dominic's earlier words. "Where no one knows me, where I don't have to put on my act…"

"It must be hard being a sex god," Angie laughed.

"It is," JJ said, in all seriousness. "But that's the image I've got to project."

"Joe Krupp's image," said Angie. "He seems horrible."

"He's tough, but he's not unkind," JJ said, and Angie was reminded of her father. "He just wants us to succeed. He's already planned a series of local gigs, and now he's trying to organize a European tour for us. And he's helped us all too."

"How?" Angie was interested: she couldn't imagine Zone's tyrannical manager helping anyone out of the kindness of his heart.

"He helped Danny's parents when they were in financial trouble and it looked as though he couldn't stay on at stage school, for instance."

"But that was to Joe's advantage too," Angie pointed out. "Danny's a great performer, and he'll be a star soon, just like the rest of you. Joe's 'help' was nothing more than a straight financial investment."

"I guess so," said JJ. "But then he helped me out when I had that trouble with the law..."

"The law? You were in trouble with the police?" Angie asked, and remembered just how concerned JJ had been when Krupp had threatened her with the police.

JJ felt Angie tense up involuntarily, and he cuddled her closer to him. "Don't worry," he joked, "I'm not a serial killer or anything like that. I'm not going to murder you out here in cold blood, miles away from anywhere!"

"I'm relieved to hear it," Angie said, and then was serious again. "What did you do, JJ?" she asked.

They stopped and sat down on a stone wall. JJ looked out into the distance. "It was just after mum and dad had been killed in a car crash, and I'd gone to live with Frank and Martha," he said. "You can't guess how screwed up I was over their death."

"I can," said Angie, and rested her head on JJ's shoulder. "My real mum died as well, remember?"

"Sorry, I forgot…" JJ said, and kissed the top of Angie's head. "Things were tough, and Frank and Martha tried to give me everything I wanted. But the caff doesn't make that much money, and it wasn't enough."

"So you went out thieving?" Angie asked gently.

"I went shoplifting," JJ said. "Once. I tried to steal a designer leather jacket. And I got caught, by a passing policeman. The shopkeeper was going to press charges."

"And Joe bailed you out?"

"I don't know what he did," JJ said. "He probably paid off the shopkeeper to keep the matter quiet. But that was the last I heard of it."

Angie smiled, and sneaked her hands inside JJ's leather jacket, and stroked his firm hard pecs. "So this 'bad boy' image isn't all hype, after all?" she teased.

"I was an idiotic little kid," JJ said. "It was a stupid thing to do, and I could have ended up with a criminal record which would have followed me around for the rest of my life."

Angie thought for a moment; it felt strange talking to someone who, if circumstances had been different, might have turned to crime. Some of her other friends were a little wild, but they never strayed from the straight and narrow, apart from the time when they smuggled bottles of wine into school parties.

"If you'd wanted the jacket so much, couldn't you have saved up for it?" she asked, hoping she didn't sound too much like a disapproving grown-up.

JJ laughed bitterly. "On what? Frank and Martha paid me a wage for working in the caff, but it wasn't much!"

"Well, you could have got another job then..." she suggested.

JJ placed a finger under Angie's chin, and raised her head so that he could look at her eyes. "Angie, I'm not as clever as you," he said. "I only scraped through school and left at sixteen with hardly any qualifications. You're brainy, and bright, and you're going to be a great journalist one day! You're going to need all the qualifications you can get!"

"You sound just like my dad!" Angie joked. It seemed odd to hear JJ talk so "sensibly" for once. JJ put a silencing finger to her lips.

"I'm serious," he said. "Don't let anything stop you getting those grades, Angie. There are hardly any jobs out there, now. I know – I looked. If it hadn't been for my music I don't know what I would have done.

"Dan, Marco, and Luke, they could probably all get other work if they had to. But all I have is my music, that's the only thing I can do. It's my only way out from another forty years on the dole, or serving egg and chips behind my uncle's counter. It's my whole life—" He looked at Angie. "—or at least it was – until I met you..."

He pulled her closer to him, kissing her, running his hands along her face, twining his fingers in her hair. Angie responded with equal ardour, her passion increasing with his. Things were starting to get decidedly steamy when Angie stopped JJ.

"No, JJ," she said firmly.

JJ smiled, and nodded. "OK," he said. "Whatever you say. I don't want to do anything that you don't want to do."

Was this guy for real? Angie asked herself. At this point most guys would have thrown a tantrum, or, at the very least, sulked!

JJ reached out and zipped up her jacket. He winked at her. "We don't want you catching cold, do we?"

"I don't think there's any chance of that," she grinned. All around them it was the middle of winter; but they were so warm together that the weather no longer mattered.

They resumed their embrace, delighting in the nearness of each other, delighting in each other's warmth. Then they jumped off the stone wall they had been sitting on, and walked off in the snow, following the path which led to the village pub.

But still there was that nagging voice at the back of Angie's mind. Telling her to make a decision. Telling her to choose.

Between Dominic and JJ.

Damn it! she told herself. *Why didn't I give in to my feelings for JJ when I first met him? Why did I have to be so clever and superior? Why did I have to judge by appearances? If I'd followed my instincts in the first place I wouldn't be in this mess now!*

*   *   *

Angie got home late that night, having spent one of the most wonderful days of her life. She and JJ had had a large and unpretentious lunch sitting in front of a roaring fire at the village pub, a beautiful oak-timbered building.

Away from the crowds, away from anyone who recognized him as the sexy lead singer from Zone, JJ seemed much more relaxed, even chatting away to the young daughter of the landlord, who was most taken with him.

By the time darkness had come and they were waiting for the bus that would take them into town, Angie had decided that she was hopelessly in love with JJ. And, what was more, she was sure that he had exactly the same feelings for her.

She had chuckled to herself and JJ had bent down to nibble her ear, and asked her what the joke was. She had told him that in a few months' time, when Zone had hit the big time, she would probably be the envy of every single girl in the country; she'd probably be known as the girl who used to go out with JJ, just before he became famous.

And then JJ had shook his head. "No, Angie," he had said. "You'll never be known as the girl who used to go out with JJ just before he became famous."

A troubled look had then passed over Angie's face, a look immediately succeeded by an expression of sheer bliss, as JJ continued: "Because you're going to be known as the girl who is going out with JJ – even though he's famous!

It's taken me a long time to find someone like you, Angie, and now that I have I'm never going to let you go. Ever."

Stephanie looked suspiciously at her step-daughter as she skipped in through the front door. "Good day?" she asked casually.

"The best!" Angie announced, and hung her leather jacket on the hook by the door.

"Who were you with?" Stephanie asked. Angie's stepmother wasn't prying, but showing a genuine interest.

"With JJ," Angie said happily.

"JJ…" The name meant nothing to Stephanie. Unlike Mr Markowska Stephanie didn't keep her finger on the pulse of popular culture; for her, pop music had ground to a halt in the late 1970s when she had been in her early twenties. "You've mentioned his name a lot in the past few days. Is he a nice boy?"

"Kind, gentle, charming," Angie said.

"Just like Dominic, then," Stephanie teased.

No, nothing like Dominic, nothing like Dominic at all!

"Someone rang for you just a few minutes ago," Stephanie told her.

"JJ?" Angie asked excitedly. He had promised to ring her the moment he got back to his hotel.

"No," Stephanie replied. "Rebecca. She said she had to talk to you urgently."

Puzzled, Angie went up to her bedroom, and punched out Rebecca's number on the telephone keypad. The receiver at the other end was picked up almost instantly. Angie asked Rebecca what the urgency was, and at the other end of the line there was an embarrassed pause.

"Look, Angie, we're best friends," said Rebecca, "and if you like you can tell me that it's none of my business..."

"It's none of your business," Angie replied, obediently.

"But I saw you and JJ yesterday in Nurse Clare's office..."

"He is so wonderful, Bec," Angie said. "Thoughtful, and funny, and so handsome, and—"

"Angie, will you listen for a minute! You're starting to sound just like me!" Rebecca snapped. Angie frowned: there was something obviously bothering Rebecca a great deal.

"Adrian and Marco warned me not to tell you," she continued awkwardly. "But you're my best friend, and I don't want to see you get hurt..."

"Get hurt?" Angie was confused. "Tell me what, Bec?"

"Well, it's probably nothing, but ... but ... but when JJ first asked you out, it was all because of a bet..."

"A bet?"

"I'm sure they didn't mean it," Rebecca went on hastily. "But the guys bet him that he couldn't get you out on a date. It was just a bit of fun: you know what boys are like. I'm sure JJ had forgotten all about it ... Angie, are you still there?"

"Yes, Bec, I'm still here." Angie's face had turned a deathly shade of white, and she was finding it an effort to keep her voice steady. There was a long pause and then she finally said, in a

162

stiff and frosty tone: "Thank you for the news, Bec. I'll see you soon."

The instant she replaced the receiver the phone rang again. She picked it up and answered it with a curt: "Yes? Who is it?"

"Hi," JJ's warm voice echoed down the line. "I've just got in this minute. I've had the greatest day with you, Angie, and I'm missing you already—"

"A bet?" Angie barked down the phone.

"What?" asked JJ, and then realized what Angie was talking about. "Oh, God, Angie, I should have told you..."

" 'Should have told me'?" Angie shouted. "No, what you should have done, you *creep*, is never to have met me in the first place. It's a shame you didn't get arrested when you tried to steal that leather jacket, because now you'd probably be inside for a very long time and out of my life for good!"

"Angie, I—"

"You've won your pathetic little bet, and I hope you're pleased with yourself. And don't give me all that rubbish about just being a poor misunderstood boy, who doesn't like the pop star image that's being thrust upon him. Save that for the teen magazines – that's if the people who fancy you can even read! Get a life, JJ – one that doesn't include me! We are finished!"

And with that Angie slammed the phone down, and fell back on to her bed, exhausted by her outburst.

And she cried and cried and cried.

14

Thank Heavens there's always Dominic, Angie kept telling herself over the next five days. She'd been a fool to allow herself to fall in love with someone like JJ, with someone so unpredictable, so totally different from herself and the people around her. It had been a silly crush, she tried to convince herself, and perhaps she had been attracted by his glamour. She'd behaved like a silly giggling schoolkid, not like the sensible and level-headed journalist she liked to consider herself.

Much better, she decided, to stay with Dominic. Just as good-looking as JJ, he was far more dependable, far more trustworthy. Going out with Dominic might be less exciting than going out with JJ, but at least Angie knew where she stood with the handsome would-be model.

However, it had been a few days since Dominic had phoned, and Angie was getting worried about his grandmother. The poor old woman must be really ill, Angie decided, and she only wished that Dominic had left her a phone number on which she could contact him. She was sure that he was going to need some emotional support at a time like this.

In the next few days she busied herself as much as possible, going into the *Recorder*'s offices every day, to work on news stories. She'd scrapped the idea of typing up her interview with JJ, of course, and had binned the cassette.

Still she was constantly reminded of the sexy singer and the boys. Whenever she turned on the local radio station their single seemed to be playing. She would tidy up her desk, and uncover the PR photo which had first introduced her to the band.

And then there were the roses. Not huge extravagant bouquets, but a single red rose, waiting for her on her doorstep every morning. There was no card with them, but Angie knew who had sent them.

Five days after she had slammed the phone down on JJ, Angie was sitting at one of the newspaper's Apple Macs, typing up a news feature, when, through the open newsroom door, she heard a commotion in the corridor outside. Rebecca was talking to someone.

"She's in there, now," she heard Rebecca saying. "But make it quick. The Principal will have a fit if he finds a non-student on college premises during the holidays."

Rebecca knocked on the open door. "Angie, there's someone here who wants to see you," she said.

Angie spun round on her chair. *JJ? Was it JJ?*

Her face fell when she recognized her visitor.

"Hi, Danny," she said.

"You don't seem so happy to see me," said Zone's young drummer.

Angie apologized. "I just thought you might have been someone else, that's all. Come on in, Danny."

Danny sauntered into the office and Rebecca discreetly closed the door behind him. He walked over to Angie's desk, and sat on it.

"I suppose *he* sent you," Angie demanded, and instantly regretted her frosty tone. She liked Danny and always thought of him as the most down-to-earth and sincere member of Zone.

"He doesn't know I'm here," Danny admitted. "And he'd probably hit the roof if he did!"

"An insult to his macho pride, I suppose."

"Angie, he's miserable," Danny revealed. "He can't write any songs, he's not singing as well as he used to. And he's driving us all nuts!"

"And whose fault is that?" Angie demanded. "It might come as a surprise to you boys, but we girls don't like being treated as something to make bets about!"

"Look, Angie, the bet began as a bit of a laugh. Yeah, sure we teased him when you wouldn't go out with him, and maybe he started out trying to prove a point. But then something happened. I've never seen him behave like this with any other girl he's been out with."

"Not even your sister?" she asked.

"My sister?"

"Yes. He told me that that was how he got to

166

know you. I presumed he'd been dating your sister. Poor girl."

Danny smiled. "Angie, when I met JJ my sister was five years old. She has Down's Syndrome. JJ used to come round and babysit so that Mum and Dad could have a night out every now and then! What's more, he'd do it for free…"

Angie suddenly felt very foolish indeed.

"And if you ever tell him that I told you that, I'll kill you," Danny joked. "Angie, he loves you and he wants you back."

"So why have you come here?" Angie asked. "Why hasn't he?"

Danny smashed his fist into the palm of his hand in frustration. "He's much too proud, Angie," he said. "JJ's a great guy, but he's also stubborn and pig-headed. And I think he's not the only one." He looked directly at Angie: it was obvious who else he meant.

"Well, if he does love me, then he has a funny way of showing it," Angie said.

"Yeah, he has," Danny agreed. "He's prepared to put his career on the line for you."

Do what?

"Didn't you ever wonder why Joe Krupp allowed us to play that New Year's Eve gig at Cuttleigh, for free?" Danny asked. Angie nodded and asked him to explain.

"The night before, JJ and Joe had one heck of a major row," Danny said. "JJ said that if we didn't do the gig then he was leaving the band. He was actually prepared to break his contract with

Krupp Promotionals: if he'd carried out his threat Joe could have chased him through the courts for years, and made sure that JJ never worked as a musician again. But Joe's no fool: he knows that without JJ there would be no Zone. So he backed down – and that's why we were able to do the charity gig at Cuttleigh."

Angie stared wide-eyed at Danny. "JJ was ready to do that – for me?"

Danny nodded. "He loves you, Angie, he's crazy about you…"

Angie remembered part of the conversation she and JJ had had on New Year's Day. *All I have is my music, Angie,* JJ had said, *that's the only thing I can do. It's my only way out from another forty years on the dole, or serving egg and chips behind my uncle's counter. It's my whole life…*

And JJ was prepared to sacrifice all that just to make her happy! He must love her, after all.

"Phone him, Angie," Danny urged. "You must have the number of the hotel Joe's put us all in. Tell him you need him, tell him you love him…"

"And why can't he tell me?"

Danny sighed. "Do it, Angie, please…"

He turned to go, and opened the door. Rebecca was standing directly behind it: she had been eavesdropping on the entire conversation. He smiled at Rebecca and then glanced back at Angie who was gazing thoughtfully at her computer screen.

"Try and see if you can talk some sense into her," he whispered to Rebecca. "I don't know who's worse – Angie or JJ. They're made for each other: they're both as proud and as stubborn as each other!"

"Angie, you've got to ring him," Rebecca said gently after Danny had left. "You know you love him."

Angie turned to Rebecca: her eyes were watery with unshed tears. "I don't know what to do, Bec," she said honestly. "How can I believe in JJ after that bet he made?"

"Like Danny said, it was a bit of fun," Rebecca said. "What does your heart believe?"

"My heart?" Angie thought. "My heart says that he is the most impossible, conceited, unthinking man in the world. And also the gentlest, the kindest, the best..."

"Well, that's what love is, Angie," Rebecca said, suddenly sounding wiser than her seventeen years. She pulled up a chair and sat down next to Angie.

"I've been out with lots of boys," Rebecca continued. "And for a few weeks I tell everyone that I'm in love with them. But they all fizzle out in the end like Adrian has, and like Rod before him. Marco will be the same, I imagine. Because I might say I love them, but I don't really..."

"Bec, you've never spoken to me like this before." Angie was genuinely touched by her friend's confiding in her.

"What I feel for them isn't love," Rebecca said. "Because I can only see a boy's good points. Aunt Lizzie once told me that you only truly know you're in love with someone when you love him not *because* of what he is, but *in spite* of what he is..."

169

Angie reflected on Rebecca's words for a moment, and remembered what Stephanie had told her had been her first impression of Peter Markowska. She'd found him insufferable at first; but they seemed to be one of the best-matched couples in the world.

"Your Aunt Lizzie talks a lot of sense for an ageing hippy," Angie remarked.

"And she's right," Rebecca added. "You know it's right."

"But Bec, it isn't that simple," Angie protested.

"You love JJ. What could be simpler than that?"

"There's Dominic," Angie reminded her. "I love him too…"

"Do you?" Rebecca asked. "Do you feel for him in the same way as you do for JJ…"

"No, but … Bec, I'm so confused … What should I do?"

"Phone JJ," was Rebecca's advice. "And if it makes you feel better, phone Dominic as well…"

"I've tried to," Angie told her. "But he's still out of town, visiting his grandmother."

Rebecca shook her head sadly. "Dominic doesn't have a grandmother, Angie."

"Don't be silly," Angie said. "She's very ill…"

"No, Angie, all his grandparents are dead. He's been stringing you along. Wherever Dominic Cairns is now, it's certainly not with his grandmother!"

"Hi, is Dominic there?" Angie asked, as the receiver was finally picked up at the Cairns' house.

"Who's speaking please?" asked Mrs Cairns.

"It's Angie."

"Angie?"

"Yes, Angie. Surely Dominic's spoken to you about me?"

At the other end of the line Mrs Cairns shook her head. "I don't think so, dear. No, I'm quite sure that Dominic has never mentioned an Angie to me before."

"But we've been going out – oh, it doesn't matter," Angie said. "Is he there?" she asked, although deep down she already knew the answer.

"I'm sorry, Angie," said Mrs Cairns. "But Dominic's down in London. It's so exciting. He's got interviews with two of the top modelling agencies. I'm so proud of him. And it's all down to his own hard work! Is there any message I can give him when he next phones?"

Angie sighed. "No, Mrs Cairns, there's no message…" She replaced the receiver.

Suddenly everything became crystal clear for Angie. Dominic's asking her to dance at the Christmas party when he'd never so much as looked at her for the past two years. His romancing of her over Christmas. His sudden interest in her father's new project. It had all been a carefully calculated plan to get hold of contacts in the fashion business.

Angie realized that she'd been taken in, deceived, well and truly hoodwinked by Dominic's classic handsome looks, his breeding, the way he always knew which wine to order with which meal.

"Kind, considerate, and selfless" Dominic had pulled the wool right over her eyes! It just proved that JJ was right, that you shouldn't judge by appearances. All the time Dominic had only been going out with her for his own selfish ends. He didn't care about her at all, didn't care that she had broken her dad and Stephanie's trust by hacking into Steph's computer; all he was concerned about was his own stupid career. And as soon as he had got what he wanted, he had taken off, and vanished for ever.

Angie felt like a complete fool, but she didn't cry. To cry would have been to waste valuable tears over that smooth scuzzball. To cry would have been to admit that she still felt something for Dominic, to delude herself that he still might love her. No, Dominic had callously taken and taken from her, and had never once given her one little thing.

Angie knew now where her destiny lay. There was only one person who had really said he loved her, only one person she had ever allowed herself to cry over. There was only one person who had given, rather than taken, only one person who had ever been prepared to lay his own future on the line for her. Angie knew now what she had to do. She picked up the phone again and punched out a number.

"Hello," she said with a trembling voice as the hotel receptionist answered the phone. "I'd like to speak to JJ, please. Yes, that's right, the lead singer from Zone. Who's calling? It's Angie – no, no, it's not Angie. Tell him, tell him, it's Babe..."

15

Two months later – March

"JJ, you were wonderful tonight!" Angie said as she ran up to JJ and gave him a great hug backstage. JJ looked around, embarrassed, at the other guys in the band. They had just finished their set and were on their way back to the dressing room, drenched in sweat. They all waved cheerfully at Angie.

"Hey, Angie, I didn't do it all on my own!"

"Sure," Angie said, and winked at the others. "Danny, Marco and Luke had something to do with it, I suppose."

"Thank you very much," Marco said sarcastically, and pecked Angie on the cheek, before moving off to the dressing room.

"Unappreciative woman!" Danny pouted as he followed Marco and Luke. "Sometimes I wish I'd never brought you two back together. Whenever you turn up at a gig you only have eyes for JJ. You never realize just how talented, and devastatingly good-looking his mates are!" He slapped Angie amicably on the back, and moved off.

"Angie, I didn't know you were in the audience tonight," JJ said, and kissed his girlfriend again. "You checking up on me?" he joked.

Angie nodded. "That's right," she said, joining in the joke. "I've read all the Sunday papers. I know what all these rock stars get up to on tour!"

"Yeah, groupies, wild late-night parties," JJ said wistfully. "Good old sex and drugs and rock 'n' roll. Well, not this rock star. Babe, at the end of a night's gig we're all so exhausted that all we really want to do is fall asleep!"

"You're really going places," Angie said, and drew JJ's attention to the sound of applause coming from the audience. "It's happening at last!"

JJ laughed. "Steady on, Angie! It's just a medium-sized town hall. It's not Wembley Arena!"

"Yet," Angie corrected him. "But the point is that we're a hundred miles away from our home town. You're assured of a great reception back home, where everyone knows you, and half of your old schoolmates are probably in the audience anyway. But to get the same sort of reception out here, where no one's ever heard of Zone, is really something!"

"I suppose it is," JJ said. "Angie, how did you get here tonight?"

"I caught the coach," she said.

Zone had been touring some of the country's small clubs and halls for the past three weeks now, and tonight was the fourth time that Angie had paid a surprise visit on the boys. JJ loved seeing her, but there was one thing that was worrying him.

"Angie, what about your schoolwork?"

"What about it?" she asked. "I'll do it on the coach back tonight."

JJ sighed. "Angie, it's great having you here, but you can't neglect your work. I left school without an exam to my name. You've got all the chances I never had. Don't screw them up just for the sake of me."

"But I love you, JJ," she said. "I want to be with you."

"And I love you too," he said, and kissed her again. "And if I had my way you'd travel with us all around the country, and I wouldn't let you out of my sight for a minute. But your schoolwork's important – you have to get your grades!"

"I've got more time now, and I'm doing fine at school," she said. "Now that I've eased up on my work for the *Recorder*, and I've given up Cuttleigh Hall."

"I hear Nurse Clare isn't too pleased about that…" JJ said. "She's almost as upset about that as Joe Krupp is about me going out with you."

"We're keeping it quiet," Angie said. "We're not harming your 'bad boy' image for the fans, are we?"

"No, but I get the impression that if he had his way we wouldn't be seeing each other. But don't worry," JJ said, and kissed her full on the lips, and ran his hand down the small of Angie's back, "because nothing in the world is ever going to take me away from you!"

"And what time do you call this, young lady?" Peter Markowska asked sternly as Angie tiptoed in through the front door later that night.

"It really is very late," agreed Stephanie.

What is this? Angie asked herself. *Some sort of welcoming committee?*

"I'm sorry," she said. "I know it's late. I've been to see JJ and the boys."

"Angie, this infatuation has got to stop," said her father. "It's ruining your schoolwork."

"It's not an infatuation, Dad," Angie said. "And it's not harming my schoolwork!"

"Then what do you call this?" Peter asked. He pulled an envelope from out of the pocket of his jacket. It was Angie's mid-term school report: her face fell.

"You used to get straight As, Angie," he said. "Now it's started to be Bs, and even B-minuses. You're taking your A-levels in three months' time; you can't afford to let your grades slip now."

Angie smiled. "You sound just like JJ," she said.

"Then he's at least showing some sort of common sense!" her father said, and then adopted a gentler tone. "Angie, I can't forbid you from seeing this ... this singer."

"His name's JJ, Dad," Angie pointed out.

"But try not to see him so often. If only for your exams."

"Yes, Dad," Angie said, sullenly. "I'm tired. Can I go to bed now?"

Peter Markowska sighed. "Good night, Angie."

"Good night, Dad, Steph."

A few minutes later there was a tap at Angie's bedroom door. She opened it to find Stephanie standing there.

"Can I come in?" she asked.

"Sure," Angie said, and invited her stepmother inside.

"He only wants what's best for you, you know," Stephanie said, as she sat down next to Angie on the bed.

"I love JJ, and he loves me," Angie said. "We need to be together."

"But at the expense of your exams?" Stephanie asked. "Even JJ can see that."

"Steph, never before have I met someone who cares so much for me," she said. "I can't bear the thought of losing him."

"So that's the problem, is it?" Stephanie said. "You think that if you can't see JJ every day he'll forget about you. Angie, from what you and Rebecca have told me about JJ I think that's the last thing he'll do..."

"Maybe," Angie said begrudgingly. "But what's really bothering Dad is the fact that JJ is in the music business, isn't it? Dad pretends to be all liberal-minded, and reads all the right newspapers and magazines, but deep down he still believes all those tabloid stories about rock stars. He still thinks that JJ's not to be trusted."

"You're his only child, Angie; he has a right to worry about you."

"He's falling into the exact same trap I did when I met JJ, and when I started going out with Dominic," Angie said. "He's judging by appearances, not giving people the benefit of the doubt … I thought Dominic was a really great, kind-hearted, selfless guy – so did Dad as well – and we all know what happened there."

"Maybe you're right," Stephanie said. "But try and spend more time on your schoolwork, as your dad suggests – if only for the next few months."

Angie nodded. "I do love JJ so much, Steph," she said. "Dad can't stop me from seeing him, can he?"

Stephanie laughed. "Ban Angie Markowska from doing something? Angie, he wouldn't dare."

Downstairs Peter Markowska had been staring at an open page of his Filofax for the past five minutes. It was against all his principles to ask favours of his contacts in the media industry, but this was a case of Angie's welfare. His only daughter was so much like her mother, always seeing things in black and white, rather than shades of grey. She took things to extremes, and never chose the middle course.

Angie was correct when she had claimed that Peter was wary of JJ because of the business he was in. But his main worry was the declining standards of Angie's schoolwork.

He knew that he couldn't stop Angie seeing JJ. But maybe he could stop JJ from seeing Angie – if only for the next five months.

He ran a finger down his list of telephone

numbers until he found the one he wanted. He dialled the number, and drummed his fingers impatiently on his desk as he waited for the connection to be made. Finally someone picked up at the other end.

"Good evening," Mr Markowska said. "I'd like to speak to Joe Krupp please..."

16

"A European tour? JJ, that's wonderful!" Angie reached out and hugged JJ for joy. The other boys were also in the dressing room, and she hugged them in turn as well. Joe Krupp came in carrying a tray on which were two bottles of champagne, and five glasses, opened the champagne with a flourish and two explosive pops, and then discreetly left again.

"The news came through this morning," JJ said, pouring out the champagne. "Five months on the road in France, Germany and Spain, supporting The Lower Depths, one of the top bands of the moment! This is really the beginning, Angie. Joe's promised us massive exposure in all the European music magazines, maybe even a couple of TV spots. When we return to England we'll be really established."

"Three cheers for Joe Krupp!" said Danny and raised his glass to their absent manager. "Even for Joe this is one major coup!"

"How d'you think he wangled it, then?" asked Marco.

"Who cares?" said Luke, and poured himself a second glass of champagne. "Just think of all those French mademoiselles, German Fraüleins, and Spanish señoritas!"

JJ glared at Luke, and then took hold of Angie's hand, and led her to a quiet corner of the dressing room.

"JJ, I'm so pleased for you, for all of you," Angie said.

JJ smiled, and shushed his girlfriend. "Angie, you do realize that this means we're not going to see each other for five whole months?"

"I could come with you," she said.

"And give up your A-levels?" asked JJ. "Uh-uh. There's no way any girlfriend of mine is going to throw away her chance of success. You think I'm going to support you when I'm rich and famous?" he joked. "No way!"

"I could always re-sit them next year," she said. JJ shook his head.

Angie shuddered. She had been so pleased by JJ's piece of news that she had never thought about its implications. It had been hard enough for the past few weeks when Zone had been on this small local tour: how was she going to cope with being separated from JJ for five months?

"I'm going to miss you so much, JJ," she said.

"And I'll miss you too," he said. He glanced over at Danny, Luke and Marco: they were pouring themselves more glasses of champagne. JJ lowered his voice so they couldn't hear what he had to say next. "The contracts still haven't been signed, you know. I could always refuse to go..."

For a second Angie was ready to say yes. She didn't think she could bear not to see the man she loved above all others for five whole long months.

But then she remembered what JJ had been prepared to give up for her two months ago at New Year. He'd been willing to lay his future on the line for her happiness then.

This was JJ's big chance, and he deserved her support every inch of the way. It was now time to sacrifice her own personal happiness for the chance for JJ to fulfil his greatest dream.

Tearfully she nodded her head. "You go, JJ," she said.

"I'll write every day," he promised.

Yeah, sure, she thought. *Every day for a week. And then maybe every two days, and then every other week. Until you meet one of those French mademoiselles that Luke's already talking about. And then I'll have lost you for ever...*

"And Angie?"

"Yes, JJ?"

"Don't worry about me being unfaithful with some silly adoring star-spotter," he said. "You're the only one for me, now and for ever. I'm crazy about you, and now that I've got you, I'd be a fool ever to let you go..."

Their farewell at the airport was probably the saddest thing in Angie's life, second only to the death of her mother. She had tried to keep smiling for JJ's benefit, but still the tears kept falling. Only a few days ago things had been so simple; now everything was going to change.

By the departure gate Krupp and the boys were waiting impatiently for JJ, who was giving Angie one final farewell kiss. He smiled down at her. "You look after yourself, you hear?" he said.

"And you too."

JJ looked over to Rebecca, who had joined Angie at the airport to say goodbye to Marco. Typically, Rebecca and Marco had split up after only a couple of weeks, and, even more typically, they had remained firm friends.

"And make sure she works hard, OK, Rebecca?" he said. "When I return as a world-famous rock star, I want to come back to an ace reporter with a string of A-levels after her name!"

He gave her one final lingering kiss, and then turned and walked smartly over to Joe and the others. Without looking round – he didn't want Angie to see the tears which were already welling up in his own eyes – he waved goodbye, walked through passport control, and was gone.

The days passed long and slowly for Angie. Just seeing JJ once, maybe twice a week, had been like a touch of sanity in her increasingly frenzied world. Astor College was gearing up for A-levels, and the entire place seemed to have been plunged in a maddened chaos of revision and study, as people tried to catch up on work which they hadn't bothered to do over the past two years, and teachers tried to cram their students with all the subjects which they thought might possibly appear on the test papers.

With JJ out of the country, Angie plunged

herself back into her school work, and her writing for the *Recorder*, as if all the studying and time she put in would help her to forget JJ and assuage the fact that he was over a thousand miles away.

This did have the advantage of improving her grades though: once again she was getting straight As and her teachers nodded approvingly. If she carried on like this, then she would be able to apply for university in the clearing system, but Angie was adamant that what she really wanted to do was work in journalism.

Mr Markowska and Stephanie kept their secret. Peter had used his contacts in the music and entertainment business to secure Zone's contract for their European tour. With JJ out of the way, Angie would be able to concentrate on her studies, and hopefully get over what he considered to be her infatuation with JJ.

It would all work out fine, in the end, he decided: Angie would forget JJ soon, and meet some nice responsible young man who came from the same background as she did.

Perhaps someone like Dominic Cairns, for instance, who, if the stories were true, was having a great time now that he had decided to leave Astor before taking his A-levels, and had moved down to London, settling into a shared flat with a couple of fellow models somewhere just off the King's Road.

Well, maybe not exactly like Dominic Cairns, Mr Markowska reconsidered. But certainly not someone like JJ. After all, he was a rock star;

and Mr Markowska knew what everyone said about rock stars...

For the first few weeks JJ wrote to Angie every day as promised. His letters were full of news of the boys' exploits. They were going down well with the locals of whichever town they played, and he gave her a list of all the places they had played, and were going to play: Paris, Lille, Lyons and Bordeaux in France; Madrid, Barcelona and Seville in Spain; Berlin, Munich, Frankfurt and Cologne in Germany; as well as scores of tiny little towns and villages she had never even heard of.

And then at the beginning of May the letters stopped coming, and he started sending her postcards instead. He was sorry, he scrawled on them in his dreadful handwriting, but things were just so busy at the moment, that he didn't have time to write long letters. They were doing a photoshoot for this magazine; the local radio station wanted to interview them; they had to make an appearance on that local TV programme.

And then the postcards stopped coming every day, and came every other day. Marco had found himself a girlfriend, he told her, who was following them on their tour; Luke had two girls going at the same time; and even Danny had had a brief fling with a slightly older woman who had fancied him as her toy boy.

And JJ? Angie wondered. Had he found himself someone on the road? Someone who would make his lonely nights warm and comfortable, and make him forget about her?

After all, Angie knew as well as anyone what they all said about rock stars.

As Angie became more and more miserable, so she threw herself more and more into her schoolwork. She was working late at night, revising in her father's study at home, when she found out that she'd mislaid one of her term papers.

She searched amongst the files which her dad and Stephanie had left on the desk, and accidentally came across a handwritten note addressed to her father. She wouldn't have paid much attention to it, and certainly wouldn't have read it, if she hadn't recognized the notepaper. It was the same sort of paper that the original press release announcing the coming of Zone had been printed on; it was headed, in bright and bold red letters, *Krupp Promotionals Limited*.

When she had read the letter she stormed upstairs to her father and Stephanie's bedroom, and slammed open the door, without bothering to knock. Her dad and Steph were still awake, reading in bed.

"What the—" began her father.

"No, what's this?" Angie demanded furiously and waved the piece of paper in the air. "You arranged that concert tour for Zone! You and Krupp are responsible for keeping me and JJ apart!"

"Angie, darling," Stephanie said. "Your father only did what's best. Aren't you pleased that Zone are becoming successful? I hear some of the English magazines are even taking notice of them..."

"That's not the point, Steph, and you know it!"

186

she bawled. "He didn't do this for Zone, he did it because he thought JJ was bad for me. He thought a rock singer from the wrong side of the tracks wasn't good enough for his precious little girl!"

"Your schoolwork was deteriorating," her father barked back angrily. "All because of JJ! Your whole future career would have been ruined! If you wouldn't give him up voluntarily I had to think of some other way!"

"How dare you!" Angie cried out. "I love JJ!"

"You're still a child, Angie. You don't know what love is!"

"No, dad, I'm not a child, I'll be eighteen in June. And I do know what love is. And I love JJ just as much as you loved Mum. Just as much as you love Steph now! And I am not going to let you drive me and JJ apart!"

She turned, and stormed out through the bedroom door. Her father leapt out of bed and followed her.

"Angie, where are you going?" he cried after her as he watched her run down the stairs into the hallway and grab her coat and shoulder bag.

"To Rebecca's!" Angie cried. "To someone I can trust!"

Aunt Lizzie handed Angie an early-morning cup of peppermint tea, and regarded her thoughtfully. Angie had arrived at her house in tears last night, and told Aunt Lizzie and Rebecca about how her father and Stephanie had conspired to keep her and JJ apart. Then she had slept, exhausted, on the futon in the spare room.

In the morning, the discussion continued. Rebecca agreed with Angie: what Mr Markowska and Stephanie had done was terrible. Aunt Lizzie, however, wasn't quite so sure.

"They care very deeply about you, Angie," she said softly.

"Well, I care very deeply for JJ too," Angie retorted. "Don't they ever think about that?"

"I'm sure JJ would say the same thing," Lizzie said. "That you must continue with your studies."

"Then he'll have to tell me so in person, won't he?" Angie said defiantly.

"You're actually going to go through with your plan?" Rebecca asked admiringly. Rebecca had been amazed at the decision Angie had come to last night. It was like something out of a romantic movie! And then she remembered what she had always said about her best friend: what Angie Markowska wanted Angie Markowska usually got!

Angie nodded, and pulled out a photocopied list of all the gigs Zone were playing in the next month. "I'm going to Europe to see Zone."

"And how are you going to get there, might I be allowed to know?" asked Aunt Lizzie. "I take it that you have no money."

"I'll hitch-hike," Angie said, even though she had never hitch-hiked in her life before.

"I see…" Aunt Lizzie looked carefully at Angie, with those spooky eyes that seemed to be able to see through anything. "Hitching through Europe alone is dangerous, especially for a young girl."

"I'll manage," Angie said, her determination hiding the doubt she felt inside. "I can look after myself."

Lizzie nodded thoughtfully, and there was an awkward silence as she continued to regard Angie. She turned away from Angie, and moved to the kitchen window. It was the beginning of May but outside the wind was howling and the rain was falling in torrents: it seemed that a major storm was brewing.

Finally Lizzie seemed to come to some sort of decision and turned back to Angie. "Are you really determined to go through with this, Angie?" she asked.

"I am. I intend to set off this morning."

Aunt Lizzie sighed and shook her head sympathetically. "You have spirit, Angie, I'll say that for you. You remind me of myself when I was your age."

"What Angie wants Angie usually gets," Rebecca said.

Aunt Lizzie took the list from Angie and glanced down at Zone's schedule. "And just where are JJ and his friends playing tonight?" she asked.

Angie consulted the list. "Berlin," she said. "But why do you ask?"

Aunt Lizzie didn't reply, but reached inside the capacious pocket of her kaftan and took out a cheque book and pen. She scribbled out a cheque, and handed it to Angie.

Angie frowned. The cheque wasn't made out to her; it had been made payable to British Airways.

"Then you'd better get down on the next flight to Berlin, hadn't you?" Aunt Lizzie said. "And don't worry – I'll think of something to say to your parents."

Angie threw her arms around Aunt Lizzie. "Thank you, Aunt Lizzie! Oh, thank you!"

Lizzie released herself from Angie's embrace.

"Don't thank me yet, Angie," she warned. "Thank me when you get back. That cheque will only buy you an airline ticket. It cannot guarantee you happiness…"

17

Whenever Angie had travelled abroad before, she had always arrived at the airport laden down with luggage, her pockets crammed full of maps and guide books. When she arrived at Berlin's Tegel airport she was carrying nothing apart from her shoulder bag (in which she always carried her passport) and a wallet containing some Deutschmarks. That was all she needed: that, and her deep love for JJ, and the overpowering desire to see him again.

So Dad thinks he can stand between me and the boy I love, does he? she thought angrily. *Well, here I am in Berlin to prove him wrong!*

She looked down at the list of Zone's gigs which she'd been clutching in her hand all during the flight. Tonight Zone were playing an opening session at the Metropol: apparently it was a big disco somewhere in the city centre. The boys were due to be on stage at 10pm.

She looked at her watch: it was still early afternoon, but she knew that JJ and the others liked to "case the joint", as they called it, checking out the sound systems and getting the feel of a place long before they were due to go on stage. With luck they would be there now.

The Metropol was in a place called Nollendorf-platz – *wherever that might be*, she thought – and she raced through the airport to the cab rank outside, where she asked one of the waiting cabbies in her faltering German to take her there.

She wished that she could speak German as fluently as she remembered JJ once saying Danny could, but nevertheless the cabbie seemed to understand her. As they passed through the wide open streets of Berlin, she wondered what JJ's reaction to seeing her here would be. He would be delighted, of course.

Or would he?

A dreadful nagging suspicion teased away at Angie's mind. What if he had found another girl-friend? What if the fact that she hadn't had a postcard from him for three days now was a subtle hint that things weren't quite the same between them as they had been? What if he didn't love her any more?

When she arrived at the Metropol, a huge grey-stone disco near the Underground – or U-Bahn – station, she was once again faced with a stage door bouncer. She recalled the trouble she had had with the bouncer at Zone's concert; but at least that one spoke English. The one at the door of the Metropol, wearing a Guns 'n' Roses T-shirt which barely covered his bulging belly, spoke hardly any English. She dived into her bag to produce her press pass: at least the word "press" was similar enough in both English and German.

The bouncer looked at the press pass and then handed it back to Angie. He shook his head.

"*Es tut mir leid, Fraülein, aber hier ist ganz privat. Sie können Zone nicht besuchen. Es tut mir leid...*" He searched around for the English words. "Sorry, miss..."

Angie stamped her foot in frustration. "But I must! I have to see JJ!" she insisted. "Tell him it's Angie."

The bouncer shook his head again, and his tone became a little more menacing: "Sorry."

Angie hadn't come so far, hadn't defied her father and Stephanie, to be stopped now. She tried to push past the bouncer, who grabbed her – not particularly gently either – and hustled her out onto the pavement.

"Let me go, you big bully!" she cried, attracting the attention of a pair of elderly passers-by who tut-tutted to themselves and hurriedly walked on by.

"It's OK," came a familiar voice, from down the street. "*Lass die Mädchen sein, Klaus. Ich kenne sie: sie ist eine Bekannte von mir. Alles ist in Ordnung.*"

The bouncer let go of Angie, as requested, and Angie looked at the person coming down the street.

"Danny!" she cried. "Am I ever glad to see you!" She rushed up to the young drummer and hugged him, knocking his back-to-front baseball cap askew. She kissed him hello.

"What are you doing here?" he asked her.

"What do you think?" she said, feeling suddenly slightly foolish. Danny was carrying a plastic bag full of cans of Cokes: the Coke machine inside the disco had run out and he had been sent out by the others to buy some more from the tiny convenience store down the road.

"Where are you staying?" he asked her, suddenly concerned.

"A little hotel down the road," she lied. The truth was that she hadn't even thought about where she was going to stay tonight, having had the vague idea that JJ would sort all that out when they met.

"It's so good to see you, Angie, here in Berlin," Danny said, and led her past the bouncer at the stage door and into the backstage area. "And JJ is going to be over the moon to see you!"

"You are the craziest, most irresponsible person I've ever met in my whole life, y'know that?" JJ said admiringly, and kissed Angie again.

"Well, you know what they say about ace reporters, don't you?"

After JJ had got over the initial shock of seeing his girlfriend again, he had wound up rehearsals for the day, and taken Angie on a whirlwind tour of the city. They had seen the famous Brandenburg Gate, visited the fantastically ornate Charlottenburg Castle built for Queen Sophie-Charlotte of Prussia, and were now looking over the panoramic vista of Berlin from the top of the 353-feet-high Europa Center in the middle of the bustling city.

"So when are you going back to England?" he asked.

"I'm not."

"What?"

"Aunt Lizzie bought me a return ticket, and my flight leaves first thing tomorrow morning," Angie said simply. "But I'm not going to be on it."

A dark shadow suddenly descended over JJ's face. "But you have to – your A-levels."

"I told you, JJ," Angie said. "I can resit those next year..."

"But won't your parents be annoyed?" he asked.

"They couldn't be more annoyed with me than they are at the moment," she said, and took JJ in her arms. "I love you, JJ, and nothing – absolutely nothing – will send me home. I'm where I want to be, with you, and I never want to be anywhere else ever again."

What Angie Markowska wants, Angie Markowska gets.

"That's ... er, that's wonderful," JJ lied.

So wrapped up in her own joy and love for JJ was Angie, that she didn't notice that he was trembling. JJ was suddenly very worried indeed.

The Berlin audience loved Zone, and JJ in particular. They screamed, they roared, they bawled out their approval, as JJ performed his sexy strut on stage. Angie watched from the wings, dancing in time to the music, mouthing the words to all the songs.

From a distance, Joe Krupp watched her, glowering evilly at her. Angie didn't care: she'd

195

beaten Joe, beaten her dad and Stephanie, beaten the whole world to be with the boy she loved. She had never felt so happy in her life.

After the show she went back to the boys' dressing room to congratulate them all. "You were great – as usual," she said and kissed Danny, Marco and Luke in turn. She looked around: JJ was nowhere to be seen.

"Where's JJ?" she asked.

Danny, Luke and Marco exchanged worried looks.

"Well, where is he, Danny?"

Danny took a deep breath. "He'll be along in a minute, Angie," he said, averting his eyes from her.

Something was wrong, Angie was sure of it. She persisted: "I want to see JJ and I want to see him now. Where is he, Danny?"

Danny looked at Luke and Marco for support. Luke nodded sadly. "Tell her, Danny," he said.

Danny took another deep breath. "He's in the dressing room next door," he finally admitted, and, as Angie walked to the door, he cautioned: "But don't say I didn't warn you, Angie…"

Puzzled, Angie walked down the corridor and opened the door to the next-door dressing room, without knocking.

JJ was there, dressed in his leather trousers and sweat-drenched shirt, which was open to the waist, displaying his smooth and muscular chest. In his arms was one of the most stunning and beautiful blondes Angie had ever seen in her life.

She and JJ were in the middle of a passionate

kiss, which they interrupted the moment they realized that Angie was in the room.

"Shoot!" JJ said, and broke away from the blonde girl. "Angie, I can explain everything!"

The tears were already streaming down her face. "It's perfectly OK, JJ," she said, trying to keep her voice steady, even though her heart had just broken into a thousand tiny pieces. "I understand everything – I understand everything perfectly."

And Angie Markowska, the girl who had travelled over a thousand miles to see the man she believed was her boyfriend, the girl who had thought that JJ was the sweetest, kindest, most unselfish person she had ever met, Angie Markowska, the biggest fool in the world, ran out into the streets of night-time Berlin, sobbing.

There was only one place she needed to go to now, and that was home.

18

Her eyes clouded with tears, Angie stumbled out of the disco and into the Berlin night. It was half-past eleven now, and a light drizzle was falling on the wide open streets. Even though it was May it was still desperately cold and a cruel wind was blowing.

Angie looked this way and that, unsure which direction to take. When she had arrived in Berlin she had assumed that she would have been staying with JJ. Now, with very little money in her pockets, and no one to turn to, she had almost nine hours before her early-morning flight left for London.

Nine hours. Alone in the night. Alone, without JJ, a thousand miles from home. Her breath caught in her throat as she suddenly realized the dangerous situation she had put herself in: a single woman, alone and friendless in a large, foreign city where anything might happen to her. It was a position that only a fool would find herself in; and then she realized that that was exactly what she was – a pathetic little fool for ever thinking someone like JJ would remain faithful to her.

A car driven by a group of jeering young men whizzed past, splattering her jeans with water from the gutter. For a second she considered going back into the disco and seeking out JJ's help. She immediately scolded herself: there was no way that she was ever going to let that louse, JJ, see how much she still depended on him, no way she was going to give him the satisfaction of knowing just how much she still needed him. By now he and his German tart were probably getting ready to go off to some trendy club, while she shivered out here in the rain and the cold.

Danny would help her, surely? Sweet, honest, reliable Danny wouldn't see her left alone in the foreign streets of the harsh Prussian city. She shook her head. Danny was JJ's best friend, and even if he did help her out – as she was sure he would – she knew that tomorrow morning he would be certain to tell JJ.

She walked off to the west, heading for the huge floodlit tower of the Memorial Church at the top of the Kurfürstendamm, the main boulevard of western Berlin. At least in the busy centre of Berlin night-life there would be people, and maybe she could find a bite to eat in one of the many sidewalk cafés she had seen when she first arrived in the city.

She allowed herself one final look behind her at the stage door, beyond which she could hear the music of The Lower Depths, the band that Zone were supporting on their tour. Neither JJ nor

Danny, neither Luke nor Marco had followed her out of the disco, and a wave of self-pity crashed over her.

Get real! she reproved herself icily. *They all think I've gone back to that hotel I told them I was staying in! They're all out of my life now – out of my life for good!*

Three hours later Angie was sitting in an up-market coffee house just off the main boulevard of the Kurfürstendamm, numbly staring at the passers-by over the rim of her third cup of coffee. It was half-past two in the morning, and the crowds out there in the street gave the impression that, whereas in other European cities people were tucked up in bed, here in Berlin they were just waking up for the night.

The café was light and airy, and filled not with the sort of lowlife she might have expected back home in Britain, but bright young things in trendy clothes enjoying a night out on the town. The lady behind the counters serving the coffees looked strangely at Angie, but didn't disturb her. It was obvious from the English girl's pale and tear-stained face that she wanted to be left alone.

Angie felt someone tap on her shoulder. *JJ? Danny?* She looked up hopefully.

"Warum so traurig, schönes Mädchen?"

Angie smiled weakly and shook her head at the boy about her age, dressed in leathers and a punk hairstyle. "I'm sorry – I don't speak German," she said.

"I was just asking the pretty young lady why

she was so sad," the punk replied. His English was almost perfect, although, like many young Berliners, he spoke with a strong American accent.

Angie shrugged and turned back to her coffee cup. "It's nothing," she said. What she thought was: *It's none of your business, creep!*

"*Ach doch*, on the contrary, it is something," the punk said and put his hand on Angie's shoulder, forcing her to turn around and look at him.

Angie shot a nervous look at the lady behind the counter, but she was serving another customer by the bar and hadn't seen Angie's unwelcome visitor. Angie looked at the rings on the punk's hand: a silver skull, and a plastic eyeball set in copper. It seemed like he was a nasty piece of work.

"A pretty girl all alone on a dark and rainy night like this," the punk continued. "Of course there is something wrong."

Angie stared the punk straight in the face, trying not to reveal just how frightened she was. He was leering at her now, and she could smell alcohol on his breath. He was unshaven, there were dark shadows under his unblinking eyes, and it looked as though he hadn't washed his hair in days.

"Look, just leave me alone, OK?" she said.

"Now you know that I can't do that," he said, and winked at her. Angie felt his hand clasp her shoulder even more tightly.

Alone in a foreign country, Angie felt as though she was living a nightmare. *Somebody help me please!* she heard herself thinking. She looked over once again at the lady behind the counter, begging her with her eyes to come to her assistance. The lady just smiled at her and continued with her work.

"Just let me be, will you!" she hissed through gritted teeth. The punk shook his head.

"You're frightening her, Wolfgang," came a female voice. "Leave her alone."

Angie turned in the direction of the voice. It had come from a young girl, about Angie's own age. Like Wolfgang she was wearing black leathers, and her hair was also dyed black and dressed in a punk style. She smiled at Angie, and took Wolfgang's hand off the English girl's shoulder.

"He doesn't mean anything," she said. Like the other punk she spoke nearly faultless English. "I hope he wasn't frightening you…"

"Of course not," Angie lied.

"Hey, sure," said Wolfgang. "I didn't mean to upset you." He smiled at her.

Well, you did! Angie thought. *You scared me almost half to death!*

The girl, who introduced herself as Grete, nodded at Wolfgang. "Go get us two coffees, OK?" she said. Wolfgang got the hint and marched over to the woman at the counter. When he was gone, Grete turned to Angie and asked her name, and then said: "OK, so what's the problem?"

Angie feigned surprise. "Problem?" she asked. "I don't understand. What problem?"

"Like Wolfgang says, a pretty girl sitting all

alone on a night like this in a café," Grete said, and smiled winningly at Angie. "There has to be something wrong."

Angie smiled back. Despite her threatening appearance there was something rather likeable about the young punk girl. "I told you, there's nothing wrong."

"So what's his name?" Grete asked bluntly, ignoring Angie's last comment.

"I beg your pardon?"

"What's his name?" Grete repeated. "I take it you're crying into your coffee over some man, *nicht wahr*?"

Angie smiled weakly. "JJ—" she started, and then corrected herself: "Jeremy."

"And you thought that this Jeremy was the love of your life?" Grete guessed.

"Something like that," Angie agreed.

"Never believe that," Grete cautioned, sounding much older and wiser than she looked. "Always believe the opposite of what men tell you—"

"But you don't understand—"

"Take Wolfgang over there," Grete said, and nodded to her companion who was bringing the coffees over to them. "He scared you – you thought he was up to no good, because of the way he looked and the way he acted—"

"I didn't," Angie lied.

"Of course you did," Grete said. "What you don't know is that Wolfgang is one of the sweetest, most gentle guys around. He wasn't coming on to you there, he was genuinely worried that you were upset." She looked up at Wolfgang, who was just placing their coffees on the formica-covered table top. "*Stimmt das, Wolfie?* Isn't that right, Wolfgang?"

"*Ja, sicher,* of course," Wolfgang replied. "I am sorry if I upset you." He proffered his hand which Angie accepted and shook.

"You see, Angie, like everybody else in Berlin, you are judging by appearances," Grete said. "Just as you believed your man when he said he loved you, when he said he had eyes only for you. Never believe what you see or hear, Angie, always believe what you *feel*."

"But, Grete, you don't understand…" Angie began. "He was so kind, so gentle … he said he loved me, that he'd do anything for me. And I'd do the same for him. We belonged together…"

"And yet he left you, *ja?*"

Angie lowered her head. "Yes, but…" For the first time she was confused. She knew what she had seen; but what did she really feel deep down? Did she really hate JJ as she had told herself as she had wandered down the streets of Berlin? Or was she prepared to forgive him, if only for the chance of feeling his warm body next to hers once more?

Grete put a hand on Angie's arm. "I understand perfectly," she said. "And when one's heart is broken, we in Berlin have only one solution for that—"

Angie sighed resignedly. She had the strangest feeling that she had just been "adopted" by this young Berlin punk and her boyfriend. "And what might that be?" she asked.

Grete smiled at her. "Why, we go out and party!"

"You are still upset, Angie," Wolfgang said, as he led her from the dance floor. "Why?"

Angie shook her head, and took her drink from Grete who had been waiting for them by the bar. "It's nothing, Wolfie," she said, as she looked back at the dancers bopping away in one of the trendiest discos in the whole of Berlin.

"You were dancing well, Angie," Grete said, as Wolfgang rejoined her and put his arm around her waist.

"I love to dance – my mother was a dancer," Angie said. "Why d'you sound so surprised?"

Grete chuckled mischievously. "With your designer jeans, and your expensive blouse, we thought that you would not want to – *wie sagt man's auf Englisch?* – to let your hair down!"

Angie giggled. "Well, that only goes to show that you should never judge by appearances, Grete!" she said, reminding the young punk of what she had said earlier.

As I did with JJ, she thought, and then reproved herself. *Stop thinking about JJ! He deceived you, left you alone in the big city. He is history, finished! I don't want to think about him ever again for as long as I live!*

"When does your plane leave, Angie?" Wolfgang asked.

Angie looked at her watch: it was half-past five in the morning, and the disco was still buzzing with life. "At 8.30," she said. "I really must thank you and Grete for looking after me…"

"We couldn't leave you wasting your time in a coffee bar, now, could we?" Grete said.

"It's more than that," Angie said. "You took my mind off … things…"

As Grete and Wolfgang exchanged a knowing look, the DJ changed the tracks on the dance floor and put on a slow ballad. Wolfgang took Angie's hand.

"One more dance before you go to the airport?" he asked.

Angie looked at Grete. "Do you mind?"

"Of course not," Grete smiled, and watched as Angie and Wolfgang started to dance and sway together to the music.

On the dance floor Angie melted into Wolfgang's arms. It felt so good to be dancing with a man again, and, even though she knew that Wolfie was Grete's boyfriend, and that he was dancing with her just as a friend, Wolfgang somehow managed to take her mind off JJ – no, off that *louse* – she had left behind at the Metropol disco.

"Are you happy now, Angie?" Wolfgang asked, as the track ended and the DJ segued into another hit.

Angie nodded. "Thank you, Wolfie," she said. "And thank Grete too. I don't know what I would have done without you."

"Dancing and music," said Wolfgang. "It can take your mind off all your troubles … Never grieve for what has gone, Angie, always think of the future…"

Angie smiled. "You're right, of course," she said. "I've got to look forward…" Suddenly she tensed in Wolfgang's arms.

"Angie, what's wrong?"

Angie heard the track the DJ was now playing, and recognized the singer's voice.

Ask me once, and I'd give you the moon,
*   For you're my best girl, and you know it's true;*
The other guys might fool you, make you dance
*   to their tune*
But, my love, I'd be lost without you.

"What's the matter, Angie?" Wolfgang asked, but it was too late. Angie was already running up the stairs and out of the disco, her eyes flooding with tears.

Oh, JJ, I do love you so! she sobbed silently. *And how can I go on when no matter where I go there will always be something there to remind me of you?*

Angie felt someone gently shake her awake. She opened her eyes and looked up to see the friendly face of the British Airways stewardess smiling down at her.

"We're almost coming into land," she said. "Will you fasten your seatbelt, please?"

Angie sat up and rubbed her eyes. "Sorry, I must have fallen asleep."

"I'll say," the stewardess laughed. "You closed your eyes as soon as we took off from Berlin. Too much partying?"

Angie didn't reply but smiled politely, and did up her seatbelt. The stewardess continued: "Since you've been asleep you won't have heard the announcement."

"Announcement? What announcement?"

"We've changed course," she said. "It's too stormy to land at Birmingham airport, so we've been diverted to London."

Angie nodded: she remembered how bad the weather had been when she had left home the previous day.

"There'll be transport laid on for you," the stewardess said, "so you don't have to worry about getting home."

As Angie had no luggage with her, she was spared the long wait by the luggage carousel, and was one of the first to pass through passport control and customs.

She walked out onto the main concourse of Heathrow's Terminal Two and looked about her. Even though it was only half-past nine in the morning, the hall was teeming with travellers dressed in their best summer clothes, and chattering excitedly about their forthcoming holidays.

Angie felt out of place amongst so much happiness. She struggled to hold the tears back as she recalled one of the last times she had been at an airport. She remembered waving JJ and the boys off on their European tour and even though she had cried then her tears had been tinged with sweetness, knowing that JJ loved her. Now her tears were tears of bitterness and regret, and anger at having been deceived by JJ for so long, and at having been made a fool.

"Angela?"

Angie froze at the familiar voice. *Not here*, she heard herself thinking, *not now!*

"Angela, it *is* you, isn't it? What on earth are you doing here?"

Angie quickly brushed the tears away from her eyes and turned around. Dominic was standing there, and he strode forward and kissed her on both cheeks.

"Hello, Dominic," Angie said frostily. Her former boyfriend was dressed casually in a white linen shirt, opened to the waist, and baggy khaki shorts. His chest and his legs were tanned a deep golden brown.

"I saw you when you were coming through passport control," Dominic said. "I was in the same queue. I tried to call out to you but you didn't seem to hear me..."

"You were on the same flight as me?" Angie asked in disbelief. She knew she had slept through most of the journey from Berlin, but even in her tired and dazed state she would still have noticed if Dominic was on the same plane as her!

"Good grief, no," Dominic said, and then grinned, rather superiorly, thought Angie. "Not unless you've just flown in from Zanzibar!"

"Zanzibar?"

"That's right," he said airily. "We were doing a fashion shoot out there ... You've heard that I'm doing modelling work now?"

"Yes I had heard," Angie said, through gritted teeth. "By the way, how's your grandmother, Dominic?"

Dominic frowned. "My grandmother?" he asked, and then the penny dropped. He affected an air of sadness. "She died, I'm afraid: we were all expecting it, of course…"

I can't believe it! How brazen can you get! Angie thought. *He's still sticking to his story!*

"And how are you, Angela?" Dominic asked, skilfully changing the subject. "I hear that you've been seeing that singer – what was his name? EJ?"

"JJ," Angie corrected him. "And no, Dominic, I am not seeing him."

Dominic smiled. "Then I'm glad," he said, and sounded as though he meant it. "Angela, I never really thanked you for getting me that list of modelling contacts…"

"No, you didn't, did you?" Angie said frostily.

"So let me make it up to you," he said. He looked at his watch: Angie noticed that it was an expensive Rolex, something Dominic would not have been able to afford only a few months ago. "There's a car waiting for me outside, but why don't we meet and do dinner tonight? I know a great place in Kensington, where only the best people go…"

"Sorry, Dominic," Angie said. "I have a coach to catch back up north…"

"The food is really first-rate, Angela," Dominic said.

"Do they serve fried egg and chips?" she asked.

"I'm sorry?"

"Never mind."

She considered Dominic for a moment. He was devastatingly good-looking, that was true enough, and it could be fun to be seen with him in a fancy London restaurant. And he seemed genuinely to want to thank her for helping him on his modelling career. Perhaps she should let bygones be bygones … it was nothing to JJ now.

Will you stop thinking about JJ!

Angie shook her head. "Thanks for the offer, Dominic," she said. "But I have to get back home."

Dominic gave her a dazzling smile, and shrugged. "Some other time then?" he said and pulled a card from out of the pocket of his shorts. He handed it over to her. "Give me a call next time you're in town, OK?"

"Sure…"

He kissed her on the cheeks again. "Well, *ciao*, Angela," he said, and walked away from her to join an equally good-looking man and a dazzlingly attractive woman who were waiting for him by the exit.

Angie saw the woman plant a kiss on Dominic's lips, and the man give him a matey slap on the back. They looked over to her, and Angie struggled to hear what they were saying.

"You're a sly one, Dom," she could just about hear the other man say above the din of the Terminal building. "Who's the cute number off the Berlin flight?"

"Someone I knew a long time ago," Dominic said. "Just an old friend."

"She seemed more than 'just an old friend' to me," the woman said as she took Dominic's arm and all three of them headed for the exit.

"You've no worries on that score," Dominic laughed. "Her old man's something big in TV – I just thought she might be useful to me, that's all…"

19

Five months later – October

"You're quite insufferable, you know that, Angie Markowska?" Rebecca said as they sat eating breakfast in Aunt Lizzie's kitchen.

"Yep," Angie said cheerfully.

"I get three Cs at A-levels, and what do you get?"

"Four As," Angie said, and added cheekily: "Sorry, Bec, I know I've let you down!"

Rebecca laughed. "I'm really pleased for you, and pleased that you've got that newspaper job," she said. "You deserved it."

Angie shrugged. "I worked hard for them," she admitted, and sighed. "But if I'd've done what I was planning to do last March, when I was being a little idiot…" She didn't finish her sentence, but Rebecca knew what she was talking about.

"You still miss him, huh?"

"I thought JJ was the most wonderful person in the world, Bec," she said. "And the minute my back is turned he's messing around with some

German girl. He made a fool of me. I loved him –
I still do. And I thought he loved me too…"

"Maybe he does," said Rebecca. "Boys are funny,
they're not like us. If someone shows them the
slightest bit of attention, if a pretty girl starts
coming on to them, then it's not their heart they
start thinking with."

"I wish I could believe you, Bec, when you say
that JJ still loves me," Angie sighed mournfully.
"But if he does, why hasn't he called me to
apologize?"

"Maybe because he's as stubborn and as proud
as you are?" Rebecca suggested and picked up the
teen magazine which was lying on the breakfast
bar. There was a small picture of Zone on the
cover: they were starting to get a name over in
England now, and JJ's face, smiling out at Angie
from a hundred magazine covers, haunted her
every day, reminding her of what a fool she had
been, and how she still loved JJ above everything
else in the world.

"My dad's trying to fix me up with the son of
one of his work colleagues," Angie laughed.

"Nice?"

Angie shook her head. "Twenty-one, a trainee
teacher and balding already!"

"Yuk!"

Angie stood up to go. "I have to rush now, Bec,"
she said. "I'm starting at the local paper on
Monday. I'm going to have to buy some new
clothes!"

"You're not leaving without me!" Rebecca said.
"If you're going to do some serious shopping then

I'm not going to be left out of it!"

As they made to leave, Aunt Lizzie came into the kitchen to clear the breakfast things.

She reminded them that they had to be back by six-thirty. Adrian, with whom both the girls had remained on good terms, was due to pick Angie, Rebecca and Lizzie up in his car. There was a big charity variety gala taking place up in Manchester, featuring some of the top stars in the country, and Lizzie, Adrian and the girls all had tickets. They'd originally been bought for Angie and Rebecca by Mr Markowska, as a reward for passing their exams, and, when he and Stephanie unexpectedly couldn't make the date, he had given the two spares to Lizzie and Adrian.

Angie and Rebecca promised that they would be back in time, and left. The minute they left the phone rang. Lizzie picked it up, and she smiled when she heard the voice on the other end.

"Ah, it's you," she said. "You want to know what seats? All right, just hold on one second."

Lizzie put down the phone, and walked over to the noteboard on the kitchen wall. Pinned to the board were the four tickets for tonight's gala; she peered at the numbers on the tickets and then returned to the phone.

"Seats J14 through to 17," she said. "And yes, I'll make sure she gets the aisle seat!"

Everyone who was anyone seemed to be at the gala tonight, and even Angie was impressed by the number of famous faces she recognized. There were actors and musicians, newscasters and politicians, as well as several big-name movie stars and high-powered Hollywood agents. There was even a member of the royal family, sitting up in the royal box away from the hoi polloi. As the gala was to be broadcast live on TV, there were scores of cameras dotted all around the theatre.

"I'm really going to enjoy tonight," Angie said as they made their way through the crush of people to find their seats.

"You deserve it," Lizzie said. "Your father's very proud of your exam success and that you've landed your trainee journalist job. Ah, here we are, Seats J14 to J17."

Angie started to move towards her seat, but Lizzie stopped her. "Nonono," she said. "You sit in the aisle seat, my dear!"

"But surely you want to stretch your legs?"

"Nonono!" Lizzie was insistent. Angie glanced at Rebecca and Adrian, who were staring conspiratorially at her. She shrugged: if Rebecca's dotty old aunt wanted her to sit in the aisle seat, who was she to argue? She settled herself down in Seat J14.

The gala began with a dazzling display of virtuoso dancing from a Russian dance troupe, and was rapidly followed by a magician, rather predictably sawing a lady in half. It was all standard variety show fare, impeccably done, stylishly presented, and Angie had seen it all a million times before. She idly wondered why Lizzie – and Adrian, who normally hated this sort of event – had been so keen to go.

Maybe beneath that wacky hippy exterior of hers there's just a boring middle-aged fuddy-duddy waiting to break out! Angie thought rather uncharitably.

The compère – a slick professional who seemed to have been on Angie's TV screen for years – introduced the first singer, a big busty blonde from the late 1960s who was making what Angie calculated was her fifth comeback. The largely middle-aged audience loved it. She was succeeded by a comic, who told the same jokes that he had been telling for the past twenty years.

Angie turned to Rebecca: this gala wasn't quite turning out to be the exciting and memorable evening she was hoping for. "If it gets any more boring I think I'm going to pass out!" she said.

Rebecca giggled. "It could get better," she said, meaningfully.

"If only we had a programme," Angie said, but Lizzie had bustled them so quickly into the theatre that neither she nor Rebecca and Adrian had had the opportunity to buy one. Angie had no idea who was on the bill at all.

Rebecca nudged her, and pointed to the stage. The comic had just walked off to rapturous applause, and the compère was now introducing the next act.

"Your Royal Highness," he began and gave the resident of the royal box an oily smile, "ladies and gentlemen. Now we have something for the younger, more with-it members of the audience—"

" 'With-it'?" mocked Angie.

"Ssssh!" Rebecca whispered. Unseen by Angie,

Rebecca winked at Adrian and Aunt Lizzie.

"Just returned from a sell-out European tour, I bring you the one, the only, the amazing—"

Oh my God, thought Angie. *I don't believe this!*

"Zone!"

The lights went down, plunging the stage into darkness, and when they came on again in an explosion of colour, Zone were standing there. The girls in the audience screamed: Zone were hot stuff!

Angie stared in horror at the stage. They were all there. Danny, still wearing his baseball cap back-to-front. Marco, his shirt still undone to the waist, showing off his pecs. Luke, still mean, moody and unshaven.

And JJ.

JJ in his leathers, smiling that sexy half-grin, strutting along the stage as though he owned it, singing in that deep masculine voice of his, tossing a cheeky grin to the young girls in the audience, promising them that, tonight, they would be the one.

JJ who she had kissed, and held close like she never wanted to let go. JJ who she had loved above everything else, JJ for whom she would have sacrificed her exams, her career, the love of her parents.

JJ who had betrayed her!

There was no doubting the impact that Zone were having on the audience. Everyone over thirty, with a few exceptions such as Aunt Lizzie, who was happily tapping her feet along to the rhythm, shifted uncomfortably in their seats.

Everyone else gazed adoringly at the new group on stage. At the foot of the stage, cameramen with their mobile TV cameras struggled to get the best shots of Zone, and of JJ as he sang his way into the hearts of millions on live nationwide TV. There was no doubt about it: after tonight Zone were destined to become the biggest stars in the country.

They sang three numbers, all raunchy rockers, and the audience erupted with applause as they left the stage.

In her seat Angie glared at Rebecca, Adrian and Aunt Lizzie. "How could you do this to me?" she hissed. "You know I never wanted to see him again in my life!"

Oh, God, JJ, I've missed you so much! she thought.

"Quiet!" Aunt Lizzie said. "There's more! They're coming back for an encore."

The four members of Zone walked back on stage, and resumed their places. Danny, Luke and Marco started playing the first few bars of a melody Angie didn't recognize.

JJ strode up to the microphone, and with a gesture silenced the applause and the wolf-whistles from some of the more uninhibited female members of the audience.

"Ladies and gentlemen," he began.

Get it right, you idiot! Angie thought irritably. *There's a princess up there in the royal box! You're supposed to address her first! Really, JJ, you've no style at all!*

"Ladies and gentlemen, thank you very much,"

he said. "It's great to be here. And I want especially to thank all of our fans who've supported us through the hard times. Those last three numbers were for you."

The boys launched into their next song, a dreamy romantic ballad.

"And this next song," JJ continued, "is for one special person. Someone I've treated badly, and someone I love more than I can say. This one's for you, Angie. Come up and join me..."

A spotlight came down on to seat J14, the aisle seat, Angie's seat. The audience burst into spontaneous applause, and the TV cameras swung round to catch Angie's expression.

"This isn't happening!" Angie whispered.

"Go on!" whispered Rebecca. "You have to go on!"

Trembling, Angie stood up, and walked down the gangway. It was a thirty-second walk: it felt like hours. All around her the audience was cheering and clapping, but Angie couldn't hear them. All she was aware of was JJ, waiting for her on stage, his arms held wide open to greet her, tears welling up in his eyes.

Finally she reached the stage and was helped up by a pair of grinning stagehands. And then there she was, back with JJ again, back with the man who she loved and who she hadn't seen in over five months. In front of millions of people on live TV!

"Welcome home, Angie," JJ breathed so that only she could hear. "I love you. I love you more than anything in the world..."

He kissed her on the lips, and put a protective arm around her shoulders. Tears were streaming down her face, as, for the first time in eighteen years, Angie Markowska was rendered speechless.

She kissed him again and then looked over his shoulder at Danny on the drums. There was a big grin on his face, and he winked encouragingly at her.

JJ smiled lovingly at Angie and started to sing, to sing only to Angie, to sing the song he had written especially for her.

You're my lover, you're my woman, you're a
  tired lonely child,
    A dreamer of dreams I know one day you'll
    find;
I'm your lover, I'm a liar, I'm nothing but a
  thief,
    I mess around, I play the field, and I waste
    half of your time.

But if you ever leave me, if you ever go away
    I'd still love you for ever, sure as night must
    follow day
You're my lover, you're my life, and I'm nothing
  but a fool
    So take me back, and hold the one who's
    crazy about you.

Backstage, Angie thumped JJ in the side.
"Ow!" he yelped. "What was that for?"
"That was for—" Angie sniffed. After JJ had

finished her song she had had to be led off-stage in a daze. "That was for being so bloody marvellous."

JJ grinned, and took Angie in his arms again. People were milling around backstage, and photographers' flash-bulbs were going off, as the press tried to capture backstage shots of the nation's latest pop sensation. JJ kissed her.

"I do love you, Angie," he said, "and you don't know how much the past few months have hurt me."

"Sssh," she said, and placed a silencing finger on his lips. "That's all in the past now. We're back together again." She kissed him once more, and then felt someone tap her on the shoulder.

"Ahem! Is this a private snogging session, or can anyone join in?"

"Danny!" Angie said delightedly, and pecked the young drummer on the cheek. "It's so good to see you again! You were fantastic out there tonight!"

JJ pulled Angie back to him. "I'm sorry for what I had to do back in Berlin," he said.

Had to do?

"It doesn't matter, JJ," she said, although the memory of seeing JJ in that German girl's arms still hurt. "You strayed once ... it doesn't matter..."

"Oh, no, he didn't!" butted in Danny.

Angie looked at Danny, and then back at JJ. "What does he mean, JJ?"

JJ glared angrily at Danny, but didn't answer.

"It was all staged," Danny said. "JJ didn't want

222

you to leave home, didn't want you to give up on your studies. But he knew that you're just as stubborn as he is. He knew that there was only one way to make you go back to England. And that was if you thought he was cheating on you!"

"Then that girl?"

"Marco's new girlfriend!"

Angie looked at her boyfriend in disbelief. "You mean you put our relationship on the line, just so that I would go back to my studies?"

JJ nodded. "Remember, I wasted my time at school. I lost my parents, Angie. I didn't want you to waste your life. I didn't want you to lose your parents too…"

"But JJ – you could have lost me for ever…"

"I had to take the risk, didn't I?" he said. "Your happiness, your future was all that really mattered to me…"

The man was unbelievable. So caring. So true. So unselfish. Angie wanted to tell him how much she loved him, how much she wanted to spend the rest of her life with him. She fell into his arms, weeping tears of joy.

"Well done, JJ," came a familiar voice. Angie looked up, to see the last person she'd ever thought to see coming backstage to congratulate Zone.

Dominic Cairns.

Dominic was as hunkily good-looking as ever. He was dressed more stylishly than Angie had ever seen him before, wearing a casual Armani jacket, Cerrutti trousers, a simple black T-shirt – and a devastatingly attractive red-head on his arm. Life down in London was going well for him, she knew: she'd already seen his face in some of the fashion magazines and the rumour was that he was going to go to the very top in the modelling business.

"Hello, Dominic," JJ said. His tone suggested that he was not at all pleased that Dominic had chosen this moment to break in on his and Angie's happiness.

"Hello, Angela," Dominic said. "It's nice to see you again."

"Hi, Dominic," Angie said.

You pig, is what she thought.

JJ looked at Danny. "Dan, join the other guys for a minute, would you?" he said. "Tell the photographers that we're about to do a photo shoot for them, OK?"

Danny nodded. "Sure, JJ. But..."

"Just do it," JJ said. "I don't want any photographers anywhere near me for the next thirty seconds."

Danny shrugged and moved off, leading the press photographers away.

When he was sure that no photographers were on hand to take a picture, JJ accepted Dominic's proffered hand and shook it.

And with his other hand punched Dominic in the face. The model fell to the floor, blood streaming from his nose.

"That was for what you did to Angie, creep!" JJ snarled, and walked away to Danny and the others.

"JJ, you shouldn't have done that!" Angie

protested, as she watched a stunned Dominic being helped to his feet by the red-head.

"I enjoyed it."

Angie laughed. "So did I. I love you so very much, JJ."

"Joe's organized a nationwide tour for us, Angie," he revealed. "Do you love me enough to wait for me?"

"Angie won't be waiting for you, JJ!"

"Dad?"

Mr Markowska had turned up backstage, along with Stephanie, Lizzie, Adrian and Rebecca.

"I thought you and Steph were away," Angie said. "What do you mean I won't be waiting for JJ? Dad, I'm eighteen now. You can't forbid me to see JJ! I love him!"

"Let your dad speak, Angie," Stephanie smiled.

"You won't be waiting for JJ," her father said, "because you're going on tour with him!"

"I'm what?" Was her father crazy or what?

"Zone are a local band," her father explained. "And you now work for the local newspaper. It seems the editor thought it might be a good idea if one of his more promising young reporters tagged along with them for the tour…"

"Dad, you used your contacts!"

"I assure you I had nothing to do with it," he lied, and winked at her.

Angie ran up to hug her father, and then returned to the arms of the man she loved. He kissed her once, and then walked up to Danny, Luke and Marco, who were waiting for him with the photographers.

As a hundred flash-bulbs illuminated the smiling faces of the biggest new band in the country, Angie felt someone tug at her sleeve. It was a young girl, perhaps her age, dressed all in black. The ID on her T-shirt identified her as one of the backstage crew.

"He's gorgeous, isn't he?"

Angie smiled. "Who? JJ? Yes, I suppose he is."

"A total hunk ... I'd hate to be the girl he marries, though..."

"Oh?" Angie was amused. "And why's that?"

"Well, he's bound to be so full of himself. Big-headed, pompous, arrogant. He probably just uses women and then throws them away like discarded tissues. I bet he's so selfish it's not true."

"And what makes you think that?" Angie asked, as she watched JJ and the boys preen themselves for the photographers.

"Well, they're all like that," she said. "You do know what they say about rock stars, don't you?"

She couldn't understand why Angie was laughing, with tears of joy running down her face.

Point R♥mance

If you like Point Horror, you'll love Point Romance!

Anyone can hear the language of love.

Are you burning with passion, and aching with desire? Then these are the books for you! Point Romance brings you passion, romance, heartache . . . and *love*.

Available now:

First Comes Love:
To Have and to Hold
For Better, For Worse
In Sickness and in Health
Till Death Do Us Part
Jennifer Baker

A Winter Love Story
Jane Claypool Miner

Two Weeks in Paradise
Denise Colby

Saturday Night
Last Dance
New Year's Eve
Summer Nights
Caroline B. Cooney

Cradle Snatcher
Kiss Me, Stupid
Alison Creaghan

Summer Dreams, Winter Love
Mary Francis Shura

The Last Great Summer
Carol Stanley

Lifeguards:
Summer's Promise
Summer's End
Todd Strasser

French Kiss
Robyn Turner

Look out for:

Spotlight on Love
Denise Colby

Last Summer, First Love:
A Time to Love
Goodbye to Love
Jennifer Baker

Point R♥mance

Look out for this heartwarming Point Romance
mini series:

First Comes Love
by Jennifer Baker

Can their happiness last?

When eighteen-year-old college junior Julie
Miller elopes with Matt Collins, a wayward and
rebellious biker, no one has high hopes for a
happy ending. They're penniless, cut off from
their parents, homeless and too young. But no
one counts on the strength of their love for one
another and commitment of their vows.

Four novels, *To Have and To Hold*, *For Better
For Worse*, *In Sickness and in Health*, and *Till
Death Do Us Part*, follow Matt and Julie through
their first year of marriage.

Once the honeymoon is over, they have to deal
with the realities of life. Money worries,
tensions, jealousies, illness, accidents, and the
most heartbreaking decision of their lives.

Can their love survive?

Four novels to touch your heart . . .

Point Romance

Caroline B. Cooney

The lives, loves and hopes of five young girls
appear in a dazzling new mini series:

Anne – coming to terms with a terrible secret that
has changed her whole life.

Kip – everyone's best friend, but no one's dream
date...why can't she find the right guy?

Molly – out for revenge against the four girls she
has always been jealous of...

Emily – whose secure and happy life is about to be
threatened by disaster.

Beth Rose – dreaming of love but wondering if it
will ever become a reality.

Follow the five through their last years of high
school, in four brilliant titles: *Saturday Night,
Last Dance, New Year's Eve,* and *Summer Nights*

POINT FANTASY

Read Point Fantasy and escape into the
realms of the imagination; the kingdoms
of mortal and immortal elements. Lose
yourself in the world of the dragon and
the dark lord, the princess and the mage;
a world where magic rules and the forces
of evil are ever poised to attack . . .

Available now:

Doom Sword
Peter Beere
Adam discovers the Doom Sword and has to
face a perilous quest . . .

Brog The Stoop
Joe Boyle
Can Brog restore the Source of Light to
Drabwurld?

The "Renegades" series:
Book 1: Healer's Quest
Book 2: Fire Wars
Jessica Palmer
Journey with Zelia and Ares as they combine
their magical powers to battle against evil and
restore order to their land . . .

Daine the Hunter:
Book 1: Wild Magic
Book 2: Wolf Speaker
Tamora Pierce
Follow the adventures of Daine the hunter,
who is possessed of a strange and incredible
"wild magic" . . .

Encounter worlds where men and women make
hazardous voyages through space; where time travel is a
reality and the fifth dimension a possibility; where the
ultimate horror has already happened and mankind
breaks through the barrier of technology . . .

The Obernewtyn Chronicles:
Book 1: Obernewtyn
Book 2: The Farseekers
Isobelle Carmody
A new breed of humans are born into a hostile world
struggling back from the brink of apocalypse . . .

Random Factor
Jessica Palmer
Battle rages in space. War has been erased from earth and is
now controlled by an all-powerful computer – until a random
factor enters the system . . .

First Contact
Nigel Robinson
In 1992 mankind launched the search for extra-terrestial
intelligence. Two hundred years later, someone responded . . .

Virus
Molly Brown
A mysterious virus is attacking the staff of an engineering plant
. . . Who, or *what* is responsible?

Look out for:

Strange Orbit
Margaret Simpson

Scatterlings
Isobelle Carmody

Body Snatchers
Stan Nicholls

Read Point SF and enter a new dimension . . .

Point Horror

Are you hooked on horror? Are you thrilled by fear? Then these are the books for you. A powerful series of horror fiction designed to keep you quaking in your shoes.

Titles available now:

The Cemetery
by D.E. Athkins

The Dead Game
Mother's Helper
by A. Bates

The Cheerleader
The Return of the Vampire
The Vampire's Promise
Freeze Tag
The Perfume
The Stranger
by Caroline B. Cooney

April Fools
The Lifeguard
Teacher's Pet
Trick or Treat
by Richie Tankersley Cusick

Camp Fear
My Secret Admirer
Silent Witness
The Window
by Carol Ellis

The Accident
The Invitation
The Fever
Funhouse
The Train
by Diane Hoh

The Watcher
Lael Littke

Dream Date
The Waitress
by Sinclair Smith

The Phantom
by Barbara Steiner

The Baby-sitter
The Baby-sitter II
The Baby-sitter III
Beach House
Beach Party
The Boyfriend
Call Waiting
The Dead Girlfriend
The Girlfriend
Halloween Night
The Hitchhiker
Hit and Run
The Snowman
by R.L. Stine

Thirteen
by Christopher Pike, R.L. Stine and others
Thirteen More Tales of Horror
by Diane Hoh and others

Look out for:

The Diary
Sinclair Smith

Twins
Caroline B. Cooney

The Yearbook
Peter Lerangis

I Saw You that Night
R.L. Stine

Pointing the way forward

More compelling reading from top authors.

Flight 116 is Down
Caroline B. Cooney
Countdown to disaster . . .

Forbidden
Caroline B. Cooney
Theirs was a love that could never be . . .

Hostilities
Caroline Macdonald
*In which the everyday throws shadows of another, more
mysterious world . . .*

Seventeenth Summer
K.M. Peyton
*Patrick Pennington – mean, moody and out
of control . . .*

The Highest Form of Killing
Malcolm Rose
Death is in the very air . . .

Son of Pete Flude
Malcolm Rose
*Being the son of an international rockstar is no
easy trip . . .*

Secret Lives
William Taylor
Two people drawn together by their mysterious pasts . . .